Journey Back To Lumberjack Camp

A Dream-Quest Adventure

JANIE LYNN PANAGOPOULOS

River Road Publications, Inc.
Spring Lake, Michigan

ISBN: 0-938682-36-9

Printed in the United States of America

Dedicated to—

My husband, Dennis Panagopoulos, and my sons Christopher and Nicholas, because they have always believed in me. And to Marilyn Knowles, my friend, who has a sharp eye for detail and a love of history.

Thanks to—

Wendell L. Hoover at Hartwick Pines State Park, Grayling, Michigan, an exceptional interpreter of Michigan's lumbering past.

Hackley & Hume Historical Site, Muskegon, Michigan.

Doug Bedell for introducing me to Maw and teaching me to milk a cow.

Contents

Chapter 1
The Principal's Office

"Let's get this straight, young man. I am Mr. Knowles, the principal here at White Pine School. I am the boss. What I say, goes! I don't want any more fighting in my school. Do you understand me? No more fighting!"

"Know-It-All" Knowles, the name everyone called him behind his back, was the toughest person Gus had ever known. Gus watched as Knowles shook his balding head back and forth, matching the movement of his finger, wagging in Gus's face.

Knowles was a giant. He had to be at least seven feet tall and weigh three hundred pounds, thought Gus. Maybe that was why he could be so tough on everybody. Everybody except Al, that is.

"Your teacher and your mother have both been in this office more times than I can count since the beginning of school. Gus, what's the rest of the year going to be like? I think this is enough, don't you?

"Do you have anything to say for yourself, young man?" Knowles asked as he squatted down and stared into Gus's face.

Avoiding the stare, Gus looked at the floor and shook his head no. This is so unfair, he thought. It's all Al's fault. That jerk. He's always giving me a hard time. Always trying to get me in trouble. If my dad was still around, he'd take care of him.

"It's not fair," Gus said, thinking aloud.

"What's that, Gus? What did you say?" demanded Knowles.

"I didn't say anything—except it isn't fair; it's not my fault. It's Al's."

"Yes, I know Gus. It's always Al's fault, or someone else's for that matter. But I have had enough. Do you hear me, young man? I have had enough!"

"Mr. Kristie, do you have anything to say?"

Mr. Kristie, who was Gus's favorite teacher, leaned against Knowles's desk and stared hard at Gus. Mr. Kristie was cool. He liked Gus and he always treated his mom really nice too.

"Well, Gus," Kristie said as he rubbed his hand over his black, bushy mustache. "The only thing I have to say is that I know you have been trying hard in class this year. You turn in your homework assignments. You participate in class discussions. And I have no complaints about your behavior, except around Al.

"I think you're a smart kid, Gus. And you have a mother who really cares about you and your schoolwork. If you think Al is causing you so much trouble, I suggest you stay away from him. You and Al are always looking for some way to pick on each other. As long as neither of you will tell us what is going on between you two, we can't help you."

Just then, the school bell rang, rattling hard against the wall, breaking the serious mood in the principal's office, and giving everyone a start. Al, who was sitting in the corner chair of the office, snickered as he watched the adults jump at the sound of the bell.

"Gus," said his mother, "Mr. Kristie is right. If you don't tell us why the two of you are always fighting, we can't help settle the problem. You two should stay as far from each other as you possibly can.

"You need to understand, Gus, that this is getting serious. I can't keep coming up here to straighten out this problem. You know my boss gets upset with me for taking time off from work. And now, I'm late again. Don't you understand? If this were an emergency, it would be different. But this is silly stuff. And you know how much I need this job. I can't afford to lose it over something as childish as fighting. It has got to stop, Gus."

Gus looked up at his mother. He understood. He understood all too well. It had really been hard for them since the divorce. All his mom did now was work. When she came home at night, she was often too tired to fix dinner. How could he tell her that Al always made fun of Gus's family and their lack of money? It would really hurt her feelings.

"You'll have to excuse me," interrupted Mr. Kristie. "I have to get to my class. The kids will be waiting. Mrs. McCarty, I wouldn't worry too much about Gus. He's a good kid. He just needs some new friends.

"How about it, Al? What do you think?" Mr. Kristie directed his question to the brown-haired, brown-eyed Al, the troublemaker who was swinging his legs back and forth, not paying much attention.

Al shrugged his shoulders and adjusted himself in his seat.

There, caught ya, thought Gus. Mr. Kristie's my bud. He really watches out for me, and he knows Al is a jerk.

Mr. Kristie smiled at Gus's mother. "Any time you would like to sit down and talk, I'll make time for you. I understand how difficult it must be for the two of you right now. I'm here if you need my help. Just call."

Annie McCarty smiled at Mr. Kristie. It seemed nice to have someone offer help and understanding.

"Gus. Al. Don't be too late. We have something neat planned for class today.

"Mr. Knowles, is there anything else?"

"No, Tom, go ahead. Your class will be waiting."

Mr. Kristie opened the office door. Smiling back at Annie McCarty, he left quietly.

"Gus, you're lucky to have a teacher like Tom Kristie on your side. He's a good teacher. You'd be smart, young man, to take his advice.

"Well, Mrs. McCarty, I suppose there is no need to hold you up any longer," continued Mr. Knowles. "I hope we won't have to do this again. Right, Gus?

"Same goes for you, Al. I know you always seem to be in the wrong place at the wrong time with this guy. I'll talk to your parents tonight at the Board of Education meeting. They'll be coming, won't they?"

"Yes, sir. They never miss a meeting when they know you want them there." Al beamed as he smiled at Mr. Knowles who smiled back in satisfaction.

"This will be the last time I speak to you about fighting, Gus. The next time, I will have to suspend you for three days. Then your mother really will have to take some time off from her job."

Gus could see the glare in his mother's eyes as she stared at Knowles. She probably disliked that guy as much as he did. Know-It-All Knowles is just another Al, only bigger. No wonder those two get along so well, thought Gus.

Gus's mother stood up, pulling on her old green coat and buttoning it to protect against the frosty day she was about to face. Gus knew she was already late for work. He also knew her boss was about as tough as Mr. Knowles.

Reaching out, she gave Gus a quick squeeze, knowing it would embarrass him if she made it look like a hug. "You behave yourself, young man, and I'll see you tonight. OK?"

Gus watched his mother leave as she closed the office door behind her.

"Well, boys, you better go to class. You won't learn much sitting around here. And I understand Mr. Kristie has something special planned for you today. Get going! And no more fighting!"

Gus looked at Al who was still sitting, scrunched down in the corner chair. He looks like a little rat, thought Gus. Al was squinting at Gus with his beady brown eyes and grinning slightly. Yep. A real rat, Gus repeated to himself.

"Let's go, boys," Knowles demanded again.

Al pulled himself up from the chair. "Thank you, Mr. Knowles, for understanding. I will really try hard to stay away from Gus so we don't get into any more trouble. My parents will be upset to know I had to come down to your office and bother you."

I don't believe this, thought Gus. He's the one causing the trouble and he will try hard to stay away from me? His parents will be upset because he had to come to the office? Give me a break. <u>His</u> parents didn't have to come here.

Gus began to feel angry again. Turning quickly, he left the office. Knowles better keep Al in there long enough so I don't have to walk to class with him.

Gus had just closed the door behind him when it opened again and Al darted out.

"Hey, Gus the mouse, wait up!"

Ignoring him, Gus walked quickly toward Mr. Kristie's classroom.

"Hey, Gus. That was pretty funny in there, wasn't it? Did you know old man Knowles is a good friend of my family? Dad knows him really well. He's pretty cool.

"Does your dad know him? Oh, I'm sorry. I forgot your dad doesn't live around here anymore."

It took all of Gus's strength to keep walking and not punch Al's lights out.

"Hey, Gus, did you see your mom jump when the bell rang? I thought she was going to hang off the ceiling. She's pretty funny. I really like her green coat, too. Where'd she get it? From the Army?"

Gus, trying to ignore the comments, began counting the squares in the tile floor of the hall. If he counted loudly to himself, he reasoned, he would not be able to hear Al.

"So Gus, where're you going now? Are you going to Mr. Kristie's class? I hear he's going to dress up again in one of his stupid outfits. I think that guy thinks he's a time traveler or an actor or something. History has gotten to him. He's really different. Maybe that's why he likes you!

"Hey, did you know he's not married? Maybe he and your mom should get together. They're both different!" Al laughed in a nasty tone.

If that jerk would just be quiet and leave me alone, thought Gus, everything would be fine.

"Gus, look! I want to show you something. Really, man, check this out. I took this from my dad's desk at home. Look!"

Gus stopped and slowly turned around. Al was pointing what looked like a small, silver gun in Gus's direction.

Gus froze.

Al clicked the little trigger. Snap.

Gus shut his eyes tightly and shuddered. When nothing happened he opened them carefully and saw an orange flame shooting from the barrel of the silver gun.

Al began laughing hysterically. "Did you think this was a real gun? It's just a lighter. Man, you must be really dumb to think I'd bring a gun to school. You can go to prison for that."

"You'd better put that thing away before someone sees it," said Gus as he turned and headed for class. I can't believe I fell for that, Gus thought to himself.

"Hey, Gussy, tell me what happens in Krissy's class today. I'm skipping. See you later, mouse man."

Gus heard the door to the boys' bathroom swing open and slam shut. Good, thought Gus. At least I don't have to worry about him in class.

Chapter 2
The White Pine

As Gus approached the door to Mr. Kristie's classroom, he could see it was still open to the hall. Inside, everyone was talking and laughing loudly. Peeking around the door, Gus saw Mr. Kristie dressed in one of his weird outfits. He was wearing a plaid flannel shirt, suspenders, and long black boots.

What the heck did he do to his mustache? Gus wondered. It was always kind of funny-looking, bushy and everything. But now it swept up in curves on each side, meeting his nose in the middle of his face.

"Hey Gus, there you are," said Mr. Kristie. "Come on in. We're just about to start. Where's Al?"

"I think he's in the bathroom," replied Gus.

"All right, everyone, quiet down. To start, can anyone tell me what I'm dressed like today? And no, not a geek!" said Mr. Kristie. The class broke out in laughter.

"For the past week we have been studying lumbering in the late 1800s. So, of course, today I am dressed like a lumberjack. And guess what else? We are going to have the privilege to listen to and sing a real lumbering song."

A groan rumbled though the class as if they were all about to get sick.

"I want everyone to take a song sheet and sing along. And if I don't hear everyone sing, we will keep going over the song until everyone joins in. All right?"

Mr. Kristie pushed the start button on his tape player and the music began. At first it was just the sound of an old fiddle playing. Then a weird ghost-like wail joined the fiddle to keep the tune going, and finally the rusty voice of an old man began to sing.

"Listen to this guy," said Mr. Kristie in an excited tone. "This man is eighty-five years old, the grandson of a lumberjack. He remembers this tune from his boyhood when his grandpa sang it to him. It's a real lumbering song from the backwoods of Michigan!

"I want you to try to guess what that weird sounding instrument is. Can everyone hear it?

It sounds something like a ghost or a cat on a back fence."

By this time everyone in the class had stopped laughing and was listening closely to the strange music. Mr. Kristie picked up his song sheet and began to sing with the old voice on the tape.

"Remember," he warned, "we can do this song for the full hour if I don't hear you all joining in."

> Come all ye gallant lumbermen that
>   range the wild wood through,
> Where the river flows and the timber
>   grows, we're bound with a jolly crew.
> For the music of the mills is stopped,
>   by the blinding frost and snow.
> And we'll range the wild woods over and
>   once more a-lumberin' go.
>
> The music of our axes will make the
>   woods resound,
> And many a lofty ancient pine will
>   tumble to the ground.
> At night, around the good camp fire,
>   we'll sing while the cold wind blows.

And range the wild woods over and
once more a-lumberin' go.

The last words of the music were just being sung by the old voice and the class when Mr. Kristie snapped off the tape player. From behind his desk, he pulled a shiny, long saw and a bow stick that is used with a fiddle.

Mr. Kristie sat down on a stool. Holding the saw and putting its handle under his left leg, he reached over and held the tip in his left hand. Then he took the fiddle stick and pulled it slowly across the flat back of the saw.

Surprised, the class began to laugh. It was the same sound that was on the tape—that weird ghost-like wail. Mr. Kristie was playing the saw!

"All right," Mr. Kristie paused. "Can anyone tell me what that strange instrument was on the tape you just heard?"

Everyone's hand shot up into the air. The answer was obvious.

"Gus, what was that instrument?"

"A saw?"

"It's not just a saw. This is a lumberjack's fiddle, or a **scratch-my-back** as they used to call it. Lumberjacks sometimes played this in camp at night when there were no other instruments available. Those 'jacks liked to play harmonicas, squeeze boxes, which are small accordions, and sometimes regular fiddles. But when none of those instruments were available, they would pound on tin buckets, strum washboards, and play the saw. This was their form of MTV.

"Gus, why don't you come up here and try playing the scratch-my-back?"

Embarrassed, Gus dropped his head to his desk. "Do I have to?" he groaned.

"Of course, you don't have to if you don't think you can do it," challenged Mr. Kristie.

Gus sat up and grinned. He knew what Mr. Kristie was doing. "All right, you win." Gus stood and sauntered over to the stool where Lumberjack Kristie sat. The class began to cheer for Gus. Suddenly, Gus was really glad Al had decided to skip class.

"The first thing you have to do, Gus, is get comfortable," Mr. Kristie instructed. "Hop up on the stool."

Gus hopped up on the stool and adjusted himself to the wooden seat.

"You all set up there?" Mr. Kristie snickered. "Oh, wait a minute. Here's a **toque** for your head. You've got to look like a lumberjack, you know."

Gus took the red knit hat from Mr. Kristie and placed it on his head. Everyone in the class began to laugh.

"Next, you take the handle of the saw and tuck it under the inside of your left leg. The teeth of the saw have to face you, so be careful."

If I let the saw slip it will really be embarrassing, Gus said to himself as he followed his teacher's directions. Man, sometimes I wonder if Al isn't right about Mr. Kristie being a little nuts about history.

"All right, Gus. Now reach over and take the saw tip in your left hand. Bend it a little so that the blade sort of looks like an 'S'."

Gus tried to bend the blade, but all it would do was make a wave. He tried again without success. The saw handle kept slipping under his leg.

"You have to press down hard with your leg," Mr. Kristie instructed.

Pushing hard with his leg on the handle, Gus held the saw steady. Then, pushing hard with his hand, he formed an 'S' with the saw blade.

"Hold on, Gus. You've got it. Take the bow and pull it slowly across the back of the saw."

Scrunching up his face, Gus concentrated on doing everything at the same time. "This is hard!" he exclaimed. Just then a long, loud whine came from the saw.

"You did it, Gus!"

Just then, Gus moved slightly on the stool. The saw began to slip, pinching his leg hard. He jumped off the stool, sending the metal saw flying with a clatter to the floor. "Ouch! It bit me!" Gus howled. The class broke into laughter and cheers for the new lumberjack scratch-my-back player.

Returning to his seat, Gus rubbed his leg where the saw had pinched him. Standing before his desk he pulled off the red knit hat and bowed to the class, all the while grateful that Al wasn't there.

As the class settled down, Mr. Kristie began to tell about the "White Pine" years in Michigan, Wisconsin, and northern Minnesota. "Can anyone tell me why we at White Pine School are so interested in lumbering?"

"Our town was started because of lumbering," several students responded quickly.

"Very good! In the 1870s most of the small towns around ours were created because they were located in prime lumbering areas."

Mr. Kristie continued. "Do you know that between 1860 and 1910 we produced more lumber than any other state, and much of it came from right here in northern Michigan?

"By 1897, our state produced one hundred and sixty billion **board feet** of lumber. This is enough to put a one-inch thick wooden floor on the entire state of Michigan—with enough left over to cover Rhode Island! That's a lot of wood!"

"Mr. Kristie, when did they start taking lumber from our area?"

"Well, here it began about 1870, just about the time of the great Chicago fire. The wood from around here helped to rebuild Chicago and make it the huge place it is today."

"Why did they want white pine?" asked a voice from the back of the room.

"Good question. One of the reasons lumbermen liked it was because it would float. We all know that there were not many roads at that time, but there were many rivers and streams all through this western Great Lakes area. These rivers and lakes were lumbering highways. The lumbermen would float their logs to sawmills to be cut and shipped to large cities by schooners.

"Mr. Kristie?" came a voice from one of the girls. "My mother said my great-great-grandmother was a cook in a lumber camp here in Michigan."

"Wow! A camp cook! Now that was a big job."

"Guess what?" called another student. "My great-great-grandfather used to run a sawmill and a lumberyard. We have some really funny, old pictures of men in cut-off pants and they all had big mustaches, curled up, just like yours, Mr. Kristie. They're standing on logs in the pictures and have big hooks in their hands. It's really wild looking."

"Wild looking! Can you imagine working in a lumber camp back then? You would have started work in late September, building a bunkhouse and **tote roads** all through October. As soon as the snow started to fall, you would be cutting logs and dragging them to the river banks to be stacked for the river drive in spring.

"Just think about living in those camps for the winter. Remember, they had no central heating and no hot running water. They didn't even have indoor bathrooms. And lumberjacks only took baths at the end of the cutting season in May. Can you imagine how they smelled?

"You know if you wanted to be warm you had to cut wood and build a fire in a woodstove. And forget any heat in the **outhouses**. You froze out there.

"Wouldn't it be fun to go back in time for just a day and see a lumber camp and the lumberjacks? My friend, the one singing the song for us on the tape, taught me an old poem about lumberjacks.

I see that you're a logger and not a
common bum,
for nobody but a logger stirs his coffee
with his thumb.
And
He never shaved the whiskers from off
his miserable hide,
for he drove them in with hammers
and chewed them off inside.

"Oh, yuck!" said some of the students. Others laughed and thought it sounded neat. Gus was thinking about it when Mr. Kristie interrupted.

"Gus, now that you are a champion scratch-my-back player, how about running down to the teachers' lounge and getting that big plate of **sinkers** I brought for a class treat?"

Gus scrunched up his face, wondering what Mr. Kristie was talking about.

"Oh, I'm sorry. You see, lumberjacks had their own language. They called it 'lumberjack lingo.' And sinkers were donuts. They were a favorite food in the lumber camps. I thought everyone would like to have a lumberjack treat today."

Everyone in class cheered Mr. Kristie. He really is a neat teacher, thought Gus as he left the room to get the lumberjack sinkers.

Chapter 3
Fire!

Gus hurried down the hall, thinking of how much fun he had in class. Mom's not going to believe I really played a scratch-my-back, he thought to himself. That Mr. Kristie is really funny, and in a weird way he makes history fun too! That dumb Al. He doesn't know what he missed today. He'll be mad when he finds out Mr. Kristie had sinkers in class. Gus laughed at the thought of having one up on Al.

All the way to the lounge Gus thought about what it must have been like to live in a lumber camp over a hundred years ago. It sounded as if those lumberjacks were tough guys.

Realizing the time, Gus started to trot down the hall toward the lounge. Wow, Mr. Kristie must be getting to me, thought Gus. I think I smell smoke.

Turning the corner of the hall, Gus could see a light blue haze coming from under the boys' bathroom door. Something was burning.

Swinging the door open, Gus saw blue smoke filling the air of the white-tiled room.

He could see Al leaning over the sink, lighting paper towels with his dad's lighter.

"Hey! What do you think you're doing?" yelled Gus.

Startled, Al jumped. "Gus the mouse! What ya doing sneaking up on me like that? Hey, check this out. These towels only take thirty seconds to burn.

"How was Krissy's class? He dress up again?"

"You better knock it off, Al, before someone catches you. I could see smoke coming from under the door. If Mr. Knowles catches you, you've had it."

"Mouse man, you forget. Knowles is my old man's buddy. He wouldn't do anything to me.

"What's the matter? You afraid something is going to happen?" Al turned and dropped a lighted towel into the white metal wastebasket. Smoke began to rise from the basket and the smell of burning trash filled the air.

"I'm going to tell Mr. Kristie." Gus turned to leave the bathroom.

Knowing he was in trouble now, Al threw down the lighter and leaped at Gus with all his might, pushing him hard against the corner of the bathroom wall. "You're not going to tell anyone, wimp. You understand?"

Just then, flames began to leap from the metal wastebasket.

"I'm gonna pull the fire alarm!" shouted Gus. He pushed hard against Al, struggling to get away. Pushing back with all his strength, Al threw Gus against the tiled wall.

Gus heard his head hit as it slammed against the wall. The jerk to his neck made him bite his tongue, and as he slid down the wall to the floor he could taste blood in his mouth. Closing his eyes in pain, he lay on the floor.

Al stared at Gus for a second. When he saw the blood coming from Gus's mouth, he panicked. Pulling open the door he darted out of the bathroom and raced down the hall.

Leaning forward, Gus began to cough. The bathroom was now filled with smoke. The wastebasket that stood beneath the paper towel dispenser had flames shooting out of it. What if the rest of the towels catch on fire?

thought Gus. What if the school burns down? They'll think I did it!

Gus struggled to his feet. His head throbbed, and he was so dizzy he could barely stand. It was hard to see through the smoke. He coughed and choked as he moved toward the burning wastebasket. He leaned down, grabbing the basket near its base to pull it away from the other towels.

Crying in pain, he fell back again, his hands burned from the metal wastebasket. I've got to get out of here, he told himself.

Gus crawled to the door and struggled to raise himself to the door handle. Unwilling to touch the handle with his burned hands, Gus slipped his arm through the large handle and pulled the heavy door ajar. Holding the door with his foot, he squeezed through the opening and stumbled into the hall.

I've got to pull the alarm, Gus told himself, as he spotted the red fire box on the wall. Grabbing for the metal arm of the alarm, he slapped it down. The frightful sound of the fire warning horn filled the halls as Gus leaned against the wall. Dizzy. He was so dizzy and sick. He slid down the wall to the floor.

Scarcely had the first blast of the warning horn sounded when classroom doors flew open. Teachers poked their heads out of their rooms and saw the smoke that had escaped into the halls. They quickly organized their classes to leave at emergency exits. There was a fire at White Pine School!

Gus lay his head on his arm and tried to breathe. Commotion was all around him. The last thing he remembered was Mr. Kristie in his lumberjack outfit bending over him and beginning to lift him in his arms.

Things got really weird then. Gus could see swirling colors all around him. It was as if he was falling into a deep hole, unable to escape the smell of fire that filled his nostrils.

Chapter 4
The Awakening

"It'll be fine, me boy. You'll be fine. Just get yourself a good breath of air. You're just a wee smoked is all.

"Why, if you were a Virginie ham, boy, you'd be pretty close to being ready to eat!"

"Tommy, now stop that," reprimanded a woman's voice. "That boy nearly lost his life out there in the **slashing** fire. Why, if ya hadn't come along when ya did, I would hate to think what would have happened to him."

"Miss Addie, you fret too much. The boy is as healthy as one of my horses. He'll be dandy in no time."

Gus rubbed his eyes as he tried to see where he was.

"Don't be doin' that boy. Your eyes might be burned."

"That boy's eyes aren't burned, Addie. Settle yourself down and stop fretting over the child."

Gus looked around the room, but it was too dark to see well. He thought he could see Mr.

Kristie standing nearby, and he thought his mother was sitting beside him on the edge of the bed.

"Look, Addie. The boy's got his eyes open. He'll be fine."

Gus tried to sit up, but still dizzy from the smoke, he eased himself down on the bed.

"Ya all right?" asked his mother.

With his eyes closed, Gus nodded his head. "Just a little dizzy, that's all."

Just then Gus heard someone enter the room. "How's that young'un? Is he gonna live?"

"Oh no." Gus knew that voice. It was Mr. Knowles. Opening his eyes, Gus edged himself up on his elbows and tried to blink away the darkness.

There before him stood the strangest sight he had ever seen. It was Mr. Knowles or what looked like Mr. Knowles. He had a huge mustache that curled up at both ends. He was wearing a red plaid shirt with what appeared to be long red underwear sticking out from the shirt sleeves and collar. He was also wearing a black vest and black pants tucked into the tops of his long boots.

"Well, there ya are, boy, back from the dead," said Knowles. "That fire was sure a nasty one. I knew we should have started a **backfire** to stop it. The darn thing almost got away from us. Then we find you layin' in a pile of slashings nearly on fire yourself.

"Where'd ya come from boy?" continued Knowles.

Afraid to be blamed for the fire, Gus blurted out, "It wasn't my fault. I didn't start that fire." His throat was sore and his voice sounded dry and raspy from the smoke.

"Of course ya didn't," cooed his mother. "We all know that. You just got caught in a slashin' fire, a burn-over."

Gus looked at his mother in the dim light, rubbing his eyes again.

"I said, don't be doin' that, boy. Close your eyes and put this nice, cool cloth on your face."

What's going on here? wondered Gus. Why is my mom calling me "boy"? And why is she talking in that funny voice? Where am I?

Gus closed his eyes and felt the cool, damp cloth across his face. It felt good.

Removing the cloth, Gus looked up to see his mother, or at least someone who looked like his mother.

"So, Miss Addie, what do ya think?" asked Mr. Kristie.

Mr. Kristie is talking funny, too, thought Gus. And why is he calling my mom, Addie?

"Well, Tommy, I believe ya are a hero."

Mr. Kristie was smiling at his mother. His grin was so big that his curly mustache poked into both sides of his nose. This guy looked like Mr. Kristie in his lumberjack outfit, but what was his mother doing all dressed up?

Gus looked long and hard at who he thought was his mother, but he could hardly believe his eyes. She had her hair all pulled up on top of her head in a way Gus had never seen her wear it before. She wore a long skirt with a big wide apron and a funny blouse with ruffles all over it.

"Boy, ya don't know how lucky ya are to have been saved by Tommy here. Ya owe him a debt of gratitude."

"Shucks, 'twas nothing, Miss Addie."

"Oh Tommy, ya should take praise when ya can get it."

"That's enough, you two," interrupted Knowles. "Since this here young'un is gonna make it, I suggest ya get back to your duties."

"Mom, what's going on? Why are you dressed like that?" Gus squeaked out of his sore, smoky throat. He began coughing. His lungs still ached from the smoke.

"Did ya hear the boy, Tommy? It sounded like he called me 'mom'. He must be worse off than we thought." Addie quickly got up and brought Gus a funny old tin cup full of cool water.

"Here, boy, drink."

Gus sat up and drank the water. It was cold and felt good on his throat.

"I don't understand," said Gus hoarsely. "Where am I?" Looking around the small room he could see he wasn't at school. He wasn't in a hospital. He wasn't even at home.

"I found you lying along the tote road. We were burning off the cuttin's from the trees we fell, and there you were," said Mr. Kristie. "That's all I know about you, boy."

"And if it weren't for Tommy here," added Addie, "you wouldn't have made it."

"Oh, there ya go again, Miss Addie."

Gus shook his head in wonderment.

Knowles's booming voice spoke up. "All I know is this here vagabond is keepin' you two from your work! Addie, ya should get goin' and **box up the dough**."

Just then the door behind Knowles burst open and there, standing in the doorway, was Al.

"Pa, where's the kid that almost got burned up in the slashin' fire? I ain't ever seen no one so stupid as to get caught in a slashin' fire before."

Gus bolted up and started out of bed after Al. "You jerk," Gus squeaked out. "You started that fire. It's all your fault."

"Hold it there, boy," said Kristie, holding Gus back.

"Let me at him!" Gus strained against Kristie's hold.

"This boy here is Alex, the Big Push's son," explained Kristie.

"The **Big Push**?" repeated Gus weakly as he stopped struggling.

"That's right, boy," howled Knowles. "I'm the Big Push around here. I run this here lumberin' camp. And you just remember that! What I say, goes!"

"Lumbering camp? What's going on? What's happened to me?" All of a sudden Gus felt scared and very much alone. Something strange had happened, and he didn't know what.

"Tommy," said the Push, "I think this boy's brains got dried out by all the smoke. I don't want no crazy young'un hangin' around camp stirrin' up trouble. He looks as big as a bear and as lazy as two. I want him out of here as soon as he's on his feet."

"Oh, come on now, boss," interrupted Tommy. "Where is your charity? The boy's been through a lot. He's just confused, that's all. Ya can't turn him out of camp just like that. Besides, where'll he go? We're thirty miles from the nearest settlement. Why don't ya let him hang around? He can do some odd jobs until the next wagon comes with supplies at the end of the week. Then, if he hasn't pulled his weight, he can at least catch a ride to town."

"Sir," said Addie in a sweet tone. "Your son Alex here could use some help in the **cookshack**, ya know. He is always complainin' about how hard he has to work. Ya know he doesn't like to stoke the fire or milk the cow. The boy can help Alex and earn his keep."

Gus sat listening and was very confused. Thirty miles from the nearest settlement? Where am I, he wondered, the North Pole? How can I be in a lumber camp? How come this lady looks like my mother? Yet, she isn't. And how can Mr. Kristie be here? Why do they call him Tommy? The only thing that made sense to Gus was that Knowles was called the "Big Push" and that Al was his son.

"All right you two bleedin' hearts, I'll give the boy a chance. Startin' tomorrow he helps Alex in the cookshack. Is that all right with you, son?" The Big Push directed his question to Al, who smiled a rat grin at his father and then at Gus.

The Push opened the door and exited with Alex following close behind.

"What a big shot! Those two sure are a pair," said Addie.

"A pair of royal pains in . . . ."

"Tommy," interrupted Addie with a giggle. "You shouldn't be talking disrespectful about the boss that way—even though it's true," Addie smiled at Tommy with a twinkle in her eyes.

"Isn't she something, boy? Miss Addie, she's no **belly burglar** either. She's the best cook north of our grand capital of Lansing and a real **corker** she is, too!"

"Oh Tommy, you're a silly man."

Gus watched and listened as the two talked and joked together. Wow, Mr. Kristie, or Tommy, and my mother?

"Well now, boy, what is it that we be callin' ya?" asked Tommy.

"My name is Gus. Gus McCarty."

"Now that's a good Irish name if ever I heard one. Wouldn't ya say, Addie?"

"Indeed, it certainly is. We Irish need all the family around us we can get, here in these northern woods."

"You, Mister Gus McCarty, may call me Addie. And this here 'son-of-Ireland' ya can call Tommy.

"Now I've got to be gettin' back to the kitchen. There is bread to be baked and pies to be made for breakfast ta-marrow."

Pies for breakfast? wondered Gus. Wow, pies for breakfast!

"I'll be seein' ya, Mister McCarty, bright and early ta-marrow mornin'. And don't be late!"

Addie opened the door, swooping her long skirt behind her as she left.

"She's a looker, that one. And don't be gettin' any ideas about her, boy. She's my girl!" Tommy smiled a grin so big that his mustache curled flat.

"I want ya to be gettin' your rest. I'll be taking the lamp with me over to the bunkhouse to make sure it's lights out for ya.

"Ta-marrow you'll be getting up before the roosters and after ta-day, ya'll need all the rest ya can get. 'cause Addie is a slave driver." Tommy winked at Gus and smiled.

Tommy reached over to the stand beside Gus's bed and lifted up a round glass lamp. The lamp had a strip of burning white cloth sticking out of the top.

"Lights out, Gus!" and Tommy leaned over and blew the flame out. Instantly the room was pitch black and the air held a bitter smell from the oil in the lamp. Gus could hear Tommy as he made his way out the door.

Gus lay back on the bed. This was the strangest thing that had ever happened to him. Maybe it was the smoke from the fire. Maybe it was the hit on the head from Al. Maybe he was dead!

No, that couldn't be right. Things were too much alive and too interesting. Gus closed his eyes which still stung a little from the smoke. It felt good not to think anymore.

Sleep was just beginning to sound like a good idea to Gus when all of a sudden he heard something that sounded like a low, deep growl. Where was it coming from? Gus held his breath, trying not to make any noise. He heard it again. It was coming from outside.

Quietly Gus snuggled down under the heavy, warm blankets of the bed and pulled them up over his head. I don't know what it is out there, thought Gus, but at least it's not in here.

Closing his eyes tightly, he drifted off into a dreamless sleep.

Chapter 5
Breakfast!

It seemed Gus had just buried his head under the covers when he heard the clanging sound of metal on metal and a loud, clear woman's voice calling out, "**Daylight in the swamp**, boys!"

Daylight in the swamp? Yeah, right, thought Gus. What a weird dream I had. It can't be time to get up yet. It feels like I just went to bed.

Gus pulled the heavy blankets from around his head and rolled over. It's still dark out! Wow! The electricity must have gone off last night, he thought. Gus stared into the darkness of the room searching for the numbers on his digital alarm clock.

Just then he heard something. Looking around he could see light beams coming from cracks in the door.

Oh, no! It wasn't a dream.

The door squeaked open and Tommy entered, carrying the glass oil lamp.

"Here, I brought ya some clothes."

Gus sat up in bed, and at the same time, he got a whiff of the best food he ever had smelled.

"Something sure smells good."

"That'll be Miss Addie's cookin'. Ain't nothin' louder than the smell of food to wake ya outta bed, is there, boy?

"I brought ya some woolie red **long johns**, Canadian **grays**, the warmest in the world they say, and a pair of boots and a flannel shirt. Those denim pants of yours will do just fine for the woods. I don't know where ya come from, boy, but those clothes ya had on your hide were sure different from any that I'd ever seen. Especially those canvas shoes. They're no good for work around here."

"Long johns? What do I need those for?" Gus picked up the red, one-piece outfit. "These look like they're way too big. They look like something I'd wear for Halloween."

"I don't know what ya do on Halloween, but around here you'll be spending most your time trying to keep warm.

"And I wouldn't be complainin' about the fit, boy. You're lucky I could get ya credit at the company store. I had to sign my name to your slip. I expect ya be payin' these things off by your good work.

"Put on those johnnies. The frost is crackin' on the ground this mornin' and snow might be flyin' by noon. And if ya got to relieve yourself, make sure ya use the outhouse behind the men's bunkhouse. The outhouse here is reserved for Miss Addie, ya understand? No men allowed!

"When ya leave out this here door, cut through the grub hall and go out the far door to your left by the stove. Outside you'll see the path to the outhouse. It's pretty clear." Tommy grinned at Gus as he moved toward the door.

"By the way, don't forget to blow out the oil lamp before ya leave. Ya don't want to burn down the cookshack, do ya?" Tommy closed the door behind him when he left.

Gus rubbed the sleep from his eyes. They didn't hurt this morning. His throat wasn't even sore. That was good, but where was he? And how did he get here?

Pulling back the heavy covers, Gus felt the cool dampness of the room. Maybe Tommy was right, thought Gus. I better put on the long johns and go find the outhouse. An outhouse instead of a bathroom. How weird!

Dressing himself in the oversized clothes, Gus slowly opened the door of his little room. Peering out, he could see it was connected to a larger room. The room had row after row of tables all set with bowls and plates. Each table had its own little kerosene oil lamp that was turned down low, giving off a soft glow.

There, at the far end of the room, Gus could see the door beside the big stove. Gus turned and blew out the flame of the lamp that lit his room and darted across the big dining room to find the outhouse.

Opening the door, Gus felt a blast of cold air. It was still dark out with a trace of pink in the sky beyond the tops of the trees. Across the clearing from the dining hall was a big building with a path that led around it to the back. That must be the path, thought Gus, as he hurried across the yard and followed it.

There were no low windows in the building beside the path. There were high ones, however, up by the roof that showed there were lamps lit inside. This must be the bunkhouse Tommy was talking about, thought Gus.

The ground along the path was worn smooth by use. And there, sitting at the end of the path was a little building. Good! That must be the outhouse, Gus reasoned.

The building had a shape of a little crescent moon cut out of the wall near the peak of the roof. A soft glimmer of light could be seen coming from the outhouse and around the cracks in the door.

Maybe someone's in there, thought Gus. He knocked softly on the door, but there was no answer.

Pulling the squeaky door open made Gus realize why they didn't keep this bathroom indoors. Yuck! What a smell!

Gus peered into the tiny room that had nothing in it but what looked like a low shelf with two holes cut in the top. The shelf was positioned over a hole dug deep into the ground. A lamp hung from a rusty nail overhead. There was a pile of leaves in one corner and an old book propped in another.

Oh no, thought Gus. I bet that's the toilet paper. He'd heard stories about how they used leaves or pages from an old catalog or book as toilet paper, but until now he hadn't believed it.

Gus really didn't want to use the little outhouse, but he didn't have much choice. It was this or the woods.

Gus was just about to leave the outhouse when he heard the same low growl he had heard the night before. It sounded very close. He peeked out the door, and then made a mad dash back toward the dining hall.

There is something around here, he thought, and I don't want to be its breakfast! Shivering, Gus noticed the cold had crept through his new clothes and long johns. I want to go back home, he thought. This isn't fun.

Gus burst into the door of the dining hall.

"Hey, watch out you crazy bum!" yelled Alex. He was standing just inside the door by the stove with an armload of wood.

"Were you raised in a barn? What are ya doing coming in a door like that? Why ain't you out helping me bring in wood for the stove?

"My pa says I'm to keep an eye on you, and if ya don't earn your keep, you'll be walking thirty miles to the settlement in the snow!"

"I'm sorry, I didn't mean to scare you. Here, let me help."

"You scare me? Never! And I don't need your help, I'm almost finished.

"Say, where'd ya get those big, old clothes? I bet Tommy got them from the company store. My pa buys my clothes in the city. See my boots. Aren't they handsome? Not like your **clodhoppers**. My pa says my boots cost him a whole lot of money!"

Gus listened and shook his head. This kid sounded just like Al.

"Hey Al, I mean Alex, did you hear that growling outside?"

"Oh, so you're a scaredy cat, too? You better be scared of Addie if she catches you out here talking. She'll box your ears for not working. You better go and find out what she wants ya to do this mornin'.

"By the way, the growling you heard out there was probably the stomachs of the 'jacks hungry for breakfast. If ya don't watch 'em they'll eat ya alive!" Alex laughed and pointed Gus to the kitchen door that joined the dining room.

Pushing the door open, Gus could see Addie surrounded by loaves of bread. There must have been fifty or more. There were pies and sinkers just like Mr. Kristie told him. Besides that, there were stacks of pancakes, tins of syrup, and plates of meat piled high and steaming.

"It's 'bout time, boy. Didn't ya hear the bell and the call?" asked Addie.

"I need ya to **break a hamstring** around here. That Alex, he's about as good as a sore toe in a tight boot."

"Addie, last night and again this morning, I heard this growling sound. Do you know what it was? It kinda sounded like . . . ," Gus cleared his throat and started to make a growling sound. "Grrr . . . ."

"Well, ya got two choices. It's either Napoleon the bear or the wildcat back in camp again."

"A bear? A wildcat? You've got to be joking!"

"I don't make jokes when I'm busy, boy. And I ain't jokin' when I tell ya it's time to get to work and stop the jabbering. We got to get ready to **jerk the hash**."

Turning to the work table behind her, she picked up two loaves of bread and put them on a tin plate.

"Here, you start placing the bread on the table—a loaf to every third settin'. When ya finish, start pouring the **black lead** and put out the **long sweetenin'**. The 'jacks like their coffee black as boots and sweet as honey.

"Don't be wasting no time. Those men will be in here any time wantin' to have their **grub**."

Gus stood for a second staring at Addie, wondering what type of language she was speaking. Black lead? Long sweetenin'? Grub?

Alex pushed his way through the kitchen door with his shoulder. "Are you always in the way? You just going to stand around with that bread in your hands doin' nothin'?"

"Now Alex, can't ya talk nice to Gus? He's new around the kitchen. Why don't ya show him what has to be done."

"I already do too much work around here. I thought he was supposed to help me!" insisted Alex.

"I want no more lip from either of you. Get to the dining hall and make ready for the men."

Alex and Gus, with their arms full of unsliced loaves of bread, went to work placing the warm loaves on the table, pouring the coffee or black lead, and putting out the sugar bowls.

Barely had they filled the last mug when the outside door was flung open and in walked every sort of man imaginable. Some were tall and husky. Others were short and wiry. They all had on heavy, wool long johns, which stuck out from under their plaid, flannel shirts. Some wore suspenders, while others wore big, thick leather belts with great buckles. They all wore high, heavy boots with their pants tucked inside.

"What's the matter with you?" asked Alex. "You act like ya never seen **bark-eaters** before.

"Ya know being new here to camp, you should get to know the men. Go greet them.

Introduce yourself. They like a good talk around the breakfast tables. Talk to them a lot. They like that."

That made sense to Gus. He walked over to the door and as each man entered, he introduced himself.

"Good morning. I'm Gus McCarty. Food sure smells good, doesn't it? Hi, how are you this morning? Sure hope you're hungry."

Each man through the door stared at Gus and gave him a mean look. These guys really look tough, thought Gus. "Hi, hope you're hungry. My name is Gus."

The last man that came through the door stared at Gus and turned, spitting something dirty and brown out the door. "Don't do no talkin' in the grub house, boy," he growled.

Just then Tommy came in. Gus was sure glad to see him. "Hi, Tommy. Nice to see someone I know. Food smells great, doesn't it?"

Tommy took Gus up by the shirt collar and backed him against the log wall. "What ya doin', talkin' in the grub house? Don't ya know you're not supposed to talk in the grub house?

"Ya ain't been talkin' to the rest of them, have ya? Have ya? Jumpin' Je-hos-a-phat, boy! Ya want Miss Addie to take the meat cleaver to ya ears? No talkin' in the grub shack. That's the rules, understand?

"There's men here from Scandahoovia, Ireland, Yankees from the East, Canucks from Canada, and Frenchmen. Ya get them all talkin' at once and work would never get done. No talkin' in the grub shack!"

"But Alex told me to," Gus protested. "He said I was supposed to greet everyone."

Tommy let go of Gus's shirt collar "That troublemaker would. You listen to me, boy. Stay away from Alex and stay close to Addie." A twinkle came to Tommy's eyes. "Ya know, I kinda wish I worked in the cookshack so I could stay close to her."

Tommy's thoughts returned to Gus. "Mind what I'm tellin' ya, boy. Stay away from Alex."

Gus straightened his shirt and shook his head. "So what else is new? First I have to stay away from Al, and now I have to stay away from Alex."

"Ya go help Miss Addie now. When the dishes are finished I want ya to come down to the barn. When I finish with the **hay-burners** I'll show you around the **bull pen**." Tommy walked away to take his place at a table.

Looking around the room, Gus counted over fifty men. Each had a mug, a bowl, a plate, and flatware. That's a lot of dishes to wash, thought Gus. He watched as the men gulped down platefuls of food. Addie walked around, pouring more black lead while Alex brought out more bowls of fried potatoes and pancakes.

"Gus," called Addie. "Make yourself useful. Bring out the cut pies."

Gus went into the kitchen and saw twenty or more pies. Loading his arms with as many as he dared to carry, he placed them on the tables in front of the men. Gus wondered how these men could eat so much food. And now they want pie?

Some of the men pulled large, dirty bandanas out from their shirts. Laying them open, they placed pieces of pie on the cloths. Then they wrapped them shut with the ends of the bandanas. The men took their packages and shoved them down the fronts of their shirts and down the tops of their long underwear.

"Oh, gross!" said Gus aloud.

Addie, who was watching over the grub hall, overheard Gus. "There's nothin' wrong with hard-workin' men takin' a bite to eat with them into the woods. At least these men work hard for their grub. It's more than I can say about you, boy."

Ashamed that Addie didn't think he was doing enough, Gus walked away. In the kitchen he found Alex carrying out pails of hot soapy water.

"Grab one and lend a hand. These are for the men to put their dirty dishes in."

Gus grabbed a large basin and followed Alex to the corner of the grub hall. The men were already lining up to place their dishes into the tubs.

Within fifteen minutes the dining hall was empty except for Addie, Alex, and Gus. Gus started to wash the dishes in the tubs of hot water and then dip them into pails of cold water. Alex dried them off and piled them back onto the tables for the next meal.

After dishes were finished, Gus started to feel like he had missed out on the best breakfast in the world. Sneaking into the kitchen, he spied a plate of sinkers, the only thing left from the huge meal. Picking one up, he started to take a bite.

"Hold up there, boy. If ya be workin' in my kitchen I need ya strong. I want ya first ta eat something of substance before ya have a sinker. Sit down. I'll get ya somethin' hot."

Wow, thought Gus. She's going to make me something special, just like Mom.

Addie returned with a large steaming bowl and held it out to Gus.

Oh, please. Don't let this be oatmeal, thought Gus.

"There ya go, boy, a nice steamin' bowl of bean soup."

"Bean soup? Ugh!"

"And I want every bit of that eaten and then ya can have the leftover sinkers. And if ya want to eat from now on, I expect ya to come to the kitchen before breakfast is served to the men.

They eat everything that isn't nailed down. Do ya understand?"

Gus understood. Either get up early and eat a good breakfast or get stuck with bean soup!

"Did ya hear me, boy?" Addie interrupted Gus's thoughts.

"Yes, Ma," said Gus.

"Ma? Why do you call me ma? I ain't no one's ma. Though, if I were, I wouldn't be ashamed to be yours," Addie's eyes twinkled at Gus.

Just then Alex pushed into the kitchen. "Oh, by the way, what did Tommy have to say to you about greetin' the 'jacks this morning? He looked real mad. You know, I can see how you got caught in that slashing fire. You are really dumb."

"Pay him no mind, Gus. You get to your eats. I know Tommy wants to show you around this mornin'."

Alex laughed at Gus and walked out of the kitchen while Gus finished his breakfast of hot bean soup.

Chapter 6
The Camp

After finishing his bowl of soup and eating a handful of sinkers, Gus felt full and sleepy.

"Come on now, Gus," said Addie. "Tommy's countin' on ya to come down to the barn. He's Barn Boss, ya know. It's his duty to care for the horses and stables. He's got a couple of hay-burners down there called Dick and Jim. Those are two fine animals if ever I saw any."

"Hay-burners? What's that?"

"They're the biggest horses you'll ever see."

Horses, thought Gus. I like horses. Gus took his tin bowl and dipped it in the hot steaming water that stood in a pot on the back of the stove and washed it clean.

"That's good, Gus. I see you're catchin' on to the rules around here," said Addie, as she went back to organizing the kitchen. "I expect ya back here in one hour to prepare for the noon meal."

Gus walked out of the kitchen to the grub hall. The tables were set and waiting for the next meal to be served. That sure's a lot of food to cook every day, he thought to himself. Mom will really be surprised to hear I worked in the kitchen. For a moment he felt guilty about his complaints at home when his mother asked him to take the clean dishes out of the dishwasher.

Outside, sunlight was shining through the woods and the camp was alive with sights and sounds. Tree stumps dotted the yard between the buildings. The largest of the wooden buildings had two chimney pipes that stuck out through the roof, belching smoke high up into the air.

The air, cool and crisp, smelled like wood burning. Across the yard, out beyond the bunkhouse, was what appeared to be a barn. Its wide doors were pulled back, open as far as they could go. Tommy must be in there, thought Gus.

For a camp in a huge forest this is sure a noisy place, thought Gus. He listened to the sound of chopping echoing and ringing through the woods. He heard the shouts of men, the rattling and banging of chains and equipment, the mooing of cattle and a growling . . . .

Growling! Gus was startled again by the sound he had heard last night and at dawn. Turning slowly around, he saw a big, hairy, black creature standing on its two back legs, pulling hard against a chain that was attached to a tree.

Wow! It's a bear! Gus stopped and stared.

"I see ya met me friend Napoleon," called a familiar voice.

Turning, Gus could see Tommy standing in the open barn door. He was wearing a leather apron over his clothes and big leather gloves.

"I been **corkin'** Dick, gettin' ready for the winter."

Gus looked puzzled.

"Ya know, putting spikes in his shoes so he doesn't go slidin' around on the icy roads. The snow will be here soon enough and then the ice. I don't want to take any chance with me boys. They're the best team of horses I ever had."

Tommy walked over to where Gus was standing and pulled off one of his leather gloves. Reaching under his apron and into his pocket, Tommy brought out a broken biscuit, left over from breakfast.

"Here. Give this **doorknob** to Napoleon. The Push wouldn't let Addie feed him more than once a day, and he's always hungry. Napoleon here, likes Miss Addie's cookin' as much as I do."

Gus took the biscuit from Tommy and slowly approached the bear near the end of its chain. He called out to Gus in low grunts and growls, straining to reach the food.

"Nothin' to be afraid of boy," said Tommy as he walked up beside Gus and took the biscuit from his hand.

"Here. Like this." Reaching out to the black bear, Tommy dropped the crumbly biscuit into his opened mouth and patted his head. The bear's paws playfully swatted at Tommy and his long pink tongue licked at Tommy's hand.

"Don't let the Push see ya feedin' Napoleon or we will both be in trouble. He thinks the bear eats too much as it is."

"How did Napoleon get here? Is he a pet?"

"A pet in a lumber camp? Ha! There's no such thing. Why, a pet would starve to death around here with all these hungry men.

"No, this here bear cub is an obligation. It was found early this spring when the land was bein' surveyed for the forty acres to be cut. The Big Push wounded its mother by accident in the woods and had to finish her off. He didn't realize that she had a cub until it was too late.

"The Push allows him here 'cause of killin' his ma. But now the winter months are comin' he'll be turned loose into the woods to find a den to sleep in this winter.

"Ya see that chain around his neck? I pounded it out for 'im to keep 'im out of trouble."

"You made that chain? Out of metal?"

"Red, hot metal over the forge. I'll show you how it's done sometime."

"This is really neat, Tommy. I've never seen a real bear before. Where I'm from there haven't been bears around for a long time."

"Tell me boy, just where are you from? Where's your ma and pa?"

Gus thought for a long time, trying to find a way to explain what had happened to him. "I don't know how to explain it. It must be a long way from here. I don't even know how I got here. And my dad isn't around anymore, and my mother has to work most of the time."

"I see. Well, there's no explainin' family trouble. Don't be worryin' about it. As long as ya do your work around here, ya got a place to lay your head."

Tommy patted Gus on the back, "Come on now. Let me make the introductions to Dick and Jim."

Gus followed Tommy back to the barn. Once inside it took a minute for Gus's eyes to get used to the dim light. But when he could see clearly, there, standing before him were the two biggest horses he'd ever seen.

"They're huge!" said Gus, "I've never seen such big horses in my life."

"They're draught horses from Iowa. A team of dapple-greys. When ya put them in their **dresses** and they throw their weight into the collar they can pull five times their weight.

"The Push wanted me to use oxen back here in the woods because of the bad roads. But I'm a horse man an' always been a horse man. That's why I was checkin' the survey land for a path for the tote road when Napoleon showed up. I needed land that would make a flat, smooth road for the horses.

"Ya see, oxen are slow, steady beasts. Sure-footed though, and they won't slip on frozen sod or rough roads. But those animals are as dumb as spit.

"Now take a team of horses weighin' in at a ton. They can pull three times the load as oxen. And a team of intelligent horses trained to the ways of the woods is an uncanny thing to watch. They can pull a sleigh loaded with logs to the river bank, keep their eyes to the road, and know the trail home again when they have dropped their logs.

"Ya know, boy, you should feel lucky to be Irish, 'cause I don't let just anyone around my horses. Especially Canocks and Frenchmen."

"Why not them?" asked Gus.

"Because a **barn boss** or a **teamster**, that's what they call me job, has to have the patience of a saint and a quiet disposition to work with animals. It's rare to find a man like that. Horses like the Irish and the big bosses like Irish teamsters 'cause we don't wear out so many whips across their backs."

"I wish I could work out here with you instead of with Alex."

"You want to be a **barn boy** and leave Miss Addie with that good for nothin' Alex? That wouldn't be very gentlemanly of ya, now would it?

"That Miss Addie, now she's an Irish lassie if ever I saw one. She's a lady in a camp of men. She needs lookin' after. That's why it's good you're in the cookshack with her."

"I suppose you're right," said Gus.

"Well, maybe if you catch on to the work around the shack I'll steal ya from Miss Addie for a while this winter to work as a **blue jay**."

"A blue jay? What's that?"

"A blue jay, a **road monkey**, or a **hay man** on the hill. It's a fella that works the iced roads and keeps them slick and smooth."

Gus scrunched up his face and patted the horse Jim.

"It's gettin' late now, boy. I want to show ya the bunkhouse before Addie needs ya again. After the grub this evenin', ya'll be movin' into the bunkhouse."

When Tommy opened the bunkhouse door, a striped cat flew out between their feet.

"I thought you said there were no pets in camp?"

"That there's Betty. She ain't no pet, either. She smells out the rats around here. Did ya see she only has three legs? She got one caught in a wolf trap, chasin' after some vermin. She's a scrapper, that one."

"She can really run for having only three legs," said Gus.

"Despite her trouble she needs no coddling. When she hunts down a rat, she's like a tiger-striped wildcat, killin' her own food and keepin' rodents out of the shacks. I wish she had a likin' for **body lice**." Tommy laughed as he pushed Gus through the door and into the bunkhouse.

The bunkhouse was a long wooden building with only a few windows up high. It was dim because the lamps weren't lit. What Gus could see and smell, however, wasn't very inviting. Double-decked bunks, filled with straw and heavy blankets, lined the walls. A bench ran alongside them.

Tommy stood on the bench with a long pole and reached up high to the ceiling where there was a trap door in the roof. He propped it open, letting in fresh air and sunshine.

At each end of the room, Gus could see large pot-bellied stoves with huge pots of steaming water sitting on them. Above the stoves hung racks that had a few pairs of dirty socks and wet mittens hanging from them.

"Home sweet home," Tommy laughed.

"This sure doesn't smell too sweet. Why can't I just sleep where I slept last night?"

"That there room is reserved for business-men and those **off their feed**. You're a workin' man now. Ya bed down with the rest of us."

Gus looked around the room. There was an old table with big tubs of dirty water. Broken pieces of mirrors were stuck up along a shelf and an old leather strap hung along the wall.

"That's where ya wash up," Tommy pointed out.

Piles of old magazines, a checkerboard, and some bottles were scattered on the benches.

"Not as nice as the room ya got now, boy, but it'll do."

"It stinks in here," said Gus, and he tried to breathe the rancid air through his mouth.

"Well, that's why they say there is so much fresh air up here in the north woods. The 'jacks keep all the stinkin' air in the bunkhouse," laughed Tommy.

"If ya think it smells bad now, ya just wait 'til all the men get in here. They been workin' in the woods all day, boy, swingin' axes. Their socks are wet. Their boots are steamin'. And they been chawin' **cut plug chewin' tobaccy** all day. It's not a pretty smell."

"Don't they take baths?" asked Gus.

"Sure, at the end of the season. I heard tell of a barkeater that once took a bath halfway through the season. He gave himself a real scrubbin' with a wire brush and lye soap.

"Ya know, they found him dead the next mornin'. It appears that he scrubbed off his top crust of dirt leavin' himself exposed to germs.

He caught his death and was gone just like that."

"You don't believe that, do you, Tommy?" asked Gus.

"Ya callin' me a liar, boy?" Tommy asked.

Gus was not sure how to take all this. "No, Tommy. I just never heard of anything like that before."

"If ya keep your ears open, ya'll hear a lot more." Tommy reached up into a crude cabinet and pulled out an old and heavy green wool blanket.

"Here. This **balloon's** for you. Your **muzzle loader** is over here, above mine."

Gus gave Tommy a funny look. "What's a muzzle loader?"

"A bunk, boy, a bunk that ya load in from the end, like a gun. Don't ya know nothin'?

"Now before ya come in ta-night, make sure ya bring in some **swamp grass** from the barn to sleep on. It will make your rest easier."

"What's swamp grass?" Gus almost hated to ask.

"Hay! Ya sure are a dandy. Ya don't know nothin' 'bout the woods life." Tommy seemed disappointed in Gus.

"Ya better be gettin' back to Addie before she has my hide for holdin' ya from your work."

Tommy reached up and pulled the pole from the sky door, letting it slam shut with a bang.

Gus threw his blanket up onto the bunk above Tommy's and left the bunkhouse to go back to the kitchen.

Chapter 7
A Full Day

The noon meal was already well on its way to being prepared by the time Gus returned to the cookshack. Alex was standing outside the back door of the shack holding several large baskets in his arms.

"It's about time. Where ya been? Goofin' off again?"

Just then, Gus heard a clanking, clomping sound from behind him.

"Haw! Haw! Let's go, Dick! Don't try bein' stubborn with me this day! Gee!"

Turning around, Gus could see Tommy bringing a large flat wagon out of the barn, pulled by Dick and Jim.

"Pull together, Jim! Haw!"

"Hey dummy," called Alex to Gus, "you better get out of the way or your friend will run you over."

Moving aside, Tommy pulled the wagon up behind the cookshack. "Lend a hand, Gus," called Tommy. "We have to get these meals out to the cuttin' grounds for the axe men to eat."

Tommy held the team still, so the wagon could be loaded.

In the kitchen, large baskets of sandwiches, cookies, and donuts were piled everywhere. Stacks of sliced bread sat waiting to be packed, along with a wooden pail of jam, a crock of butter, condensed milk, long sweetenin', and a work box full of utensils.

Gus took a basket to the wagon. As Tommy held the horses' reins, he gave orders about packing a balanced load.

Addie brought out two huge coffee pots that were still hot and steaming. Those 'jacks sure like their black lead, thought Gus.

"Be careful, boy," urged Addie. "These pots are hotter than fire itself. It's easy to get scalded if they spill." Addie struggled to slide the pots onto the wagon bed with Gus's help.

Dick and Jim pawed at the ground with their hooves as they waited patiently to pull their load into the woods.

"Addie, can I go out to deliver lunches?" asked Gus.

"**Dinnerin' out**? That's my job," interrupted Alex. "I do that with Tommy. You have to stay here and help serve the rest of the men that don't swing axes. Anyway, the men don't like greenhorns in the woods. It brings them bad luck."

Just then Addie disappeared inside the door to the cookshack and reappeared with another basket. She shoved it into Alex's arms and directed him to get moving.

Alex jumped onto the back of the wagon and threw himself up over the bench seat beside Tommy. Looking back at Gus, he flashed a grin.

Tommy slapped the back of the horses with the reins and the wagon slowly pulled away. The horses needed no guiding. Lifting their feet high into the air at each step, they started down the well-trampled tote road. The wagon squeaked and clanked as it disappeared around the curve into the woods.

At noontime only a handful of men came to eat in the cookshack. This time, Gus was careful not to speak to any of the men as he poured the black lead and brought out great pots of stew.

After the meal Gus washed the tin dishes in steaming tubs of soapy water. Then he dried them and set them on the table for supper.

Addie watched in satisfaction as Gus completed his chores. "Now you're finished, I have work for ya in the kitchen," said Addie, handing him an empty flour bag.

"Here, tie it around ya. It's your apron. There are **pratties** to peel."

Sitting on the kitchen floor were two bushels of potatoes and a big iron pot filled with cold water.

"Peel the pratties and put them in the pot," Addie instructed.

Gus sat down on an old crate and began peeling potatoes, one at a time, over and over again.

"Addie, don't you get tired of working like this?" Gus asked.

Addie, kneading bread dough on a long wooden table, looked up at Gus and smiled. "What is there to life, boy, if ya can't work? Ya know, me dear ol' ma once told me, God rest her soul, that the only thing ya gonna get out of life is a good meal. I feel like I am doin' a great service to these men by givin' 'em just that."

"You mean you want to do this for the rest of your life?"

"Well, now, come to think of it, I wouldn't mind settlin' down someplace and home-steadin' with a good hard-workin' man. And raise myself a houseful of children."

"A hard-working man like Tommy, maybe?" Gus joked.

Addie looked at Gus with a real twinkle in her eyes as she kneaded the bread. As quick as a heartbeat, Addie reached over and picked up a damp towel from the bread board and flung it across the table at Gus's head.

Gus ducked and laughed.

"You be mindin' your own business, Gus McCarty," said Addie as she went back to kneading the bread, this time with a big smile on her face.

Gus and Addie worked all afternoon together, stirring, baking, chopping and peeling.

Alex came in late in the afternoon carrying the empty baskets and dishes from the crew's noon meal. Seeing Gus elbow-deep in potato peelings, he gave him a smart-alecky grin.

"Now that's what I like to see," said Alex, "a cook's helper, helping!"

"You button your lip, Alex," insisted Addie. "Gus here has been working twice as fast as you ever did. And furthermore, when ya finish washin' all the dishes from the choppin' crew's dinner, I want ya to chop and stack some more wood for the oven."

Alex groaned and gave Gus a dirty look. "I thought he was supposed to do the wood!"

"You leave him be, young man. I have another job for him, too." snapped Addie.

"It's near time, Gus," said Addie as she looked up at the old box clock that sat on the shelf. "I want ya to be puttin' the pratties on the back of the stove to start a-boilin'. Take off your apron and follow me to the barn. Just set those peelin's aside. I'll be usin' them for soup ta-marrow."

Addie threw a shawl around her shoulders and picked up a tin pail. Alex, who was now washing dishes, started to laugh. "Have fun Gus."

Closing the cookshack door behind him, Gus wondered what Alex meant. Hurrying to keep up with Addie, Gus noticed that she walked at a pace a jogger would have trouble keeping up with. She made her way to the barn, swinging her pail as she went.

Inside the barn, Gus saw Tommy rubbing down Dick and Jim and putting bags full of feed around their heads to eat. "Hello Tommy," called Gus. Tommy motioned Gus to keep up with Addie, who marched past the horse stalls to the back of the barn. There, inside a fenced area were two cows.

"Boy?" asked Addie, "do ya know how to milk?"

"Milk?" asked Gus horrified. "You mean milk a cow?"

"Well, she's not meanin' to milk my horses," called Tommy who had followed the pair.

"You want me to milk both cows?"

"If ya can get milk out of both of them, Gus, you're a miracle worker. This is Maw and the other one is her son," said Addie as she pointed the cows out to Gus.

Gus looked at the white-and-black spotted cows, who were both nearly the same size.

"I'll get them apart for ya Addie," said Tommy. "Ya see, boy, even though her calf is near her size, he still tries to nurse, to get her milk. He doesn't like that someone else wants it too."

Tommy jumped over the gate into the fenced area. Running after the calf, he grabbed hold of its tail and pulled it in the opposite direction of its mother. Frightened, the calf turned and ran out a door into another fenced pen. Tommy then threw a gate shut between the two.

The cow named Maw stood in the corner watching Tommy carefully. When Tommy got close to her, she ran to the opposite side of the barn.

"Now come on, Maw. Show Gus what a nice girl ya can be."

The calf mooed loudly and his mother replied. Tommy picked up a handful of clean hay and waved it in front of Maw.

"This one here is a dumb animal. All she knows is to give milk and eat," laughed Tommy.

The cow reached out with her nose and lifted her head, smelling the hay. Tommy poked it out farther in front of her to nibble on. As she moved toward the hay, he grabbed the rope that hung around her neck and led her over to the manger. Then he tied her head between two poles and filled the manger with hay and grain.

"There ya go, girl, it's time." Tommy looked at Addie and smiled. "There's Maw for ya, Addie."

Addie came around behind the cow and Gus followed far behind, in case the cow decided to kick.

Just as Gus walked around her, she lifted her tail.

"Watch it," called Tommy. "She's got business to do."

"Oh gross!" Gus turned his head away. Addie and Tommy laughed at him.

Tommy took his shovel and shoveled the manure away. Addie placed a small, three-legged stool beside the cow.

"First, ya have to let her know you're friendly like. Don't go makin' no sudden moves 'til she gets to know ya. And don't get too near her back legs. This one has been known to kick."

"Ya can ask Alex about that," Tommy said with a smile.

Addie sat down on the little stool and placed her tin pail under the cow. Reaching out she grabbed the cow's udder.

"Can ya see how she's gettin' full?" The udder of the cow hung loose and heavy from the cow's stomach.

"Oh yuck. Do I have to do this?" pleaded Gus.

"Ya most certainly do. Now watch what I do and then ya can finish," said Addie. "A boy your age should have been milkin' long ago."

Addie grabbed at the cow and pulled. "First ya squeeze, then ya pull down. Squeeze and pull down. Squeeze and pull down."

Addie turned to the cow and rested her head against its side. With both her hands she squeezed and pulled, squeezed and pulled. The sound of spraying milk could be heard in the pail.

"Wow! Look at that!" exclaimed Gus.

Phsss . . . phsss . . . phsss . . . phsss. The milk hit the tin pail as Addie squeezed and pulled. "I can sure tell ya weren't raised on a farm, Gus," said Addie as she worked.

Just then Gus felt something nudge up against the back of his legs. Jumping back with a start, he turned to see Betty, the three-legged cat, brushing up against him. Gus reached down to pet the cat, who darted away when she saw his hand coming toward her.

"I wouldn't be doin' that if I were you. She ain't no pet," said Tommy. "She is only here because she heard the milk in the bucket. You just step aside and watch what happens."

Gus stepped back and Betty crept up and sat beside Addie. Addie smiled at the cat who sat back wobbling, trying to balance on her good hind leg and her stub. She meowed and sniffed the air.

Gus watched with surprise as Addie squirted milk right into Betty's face. The cat opened her mouth as the milk splashed her. Swatting at the stream of milk, she licked and licked and licked, while wobbling back and forth. After a thorough soaking, she jumped back and shook herself. Then she sat down to lick the milk from her fur.

Gus had never seen anything like that before, and he was surprised. Addie and Tommy laughed at the poor, three-legged cat as she lost her balance and fell backward, still licking her fur.

"Now it's your turn, Gus," said Addie. She stood and moved away from the stool.

All of a sudden Gus was serious. "My hands are cold. Does it matter?" he asked as h e rubbed them together.

"No, it doesn't matter to Maw the least bit," said Addie with a smile.

Gus sat down on the short stool and put his head up against Maw. Reaching forward he pulled at the cow—squeeze and pull, squeeze and pull.

"It's not working," said Gus.

"You're tryin' too hard," said Tommy. "It's as **easy as fallin' off a log**. Pull easy and it'll work."

Gus squeezed lightly and pulled. Phsss. Into the pail it went. Squeeze and pull. Phsss.

'This is fun." said Gus.

"I'm glad ya like it, boy. It'll be your job every mornin' before breakfast and every evenin' before supper," said Addie.

With that, Addie walked off with Tommy by the horse stalls where they talked quietly.

Gus milked the cow until there was no more milk to give. In ten minutes he had filled the pail almost to the top

Looking around, Gus could see Addie and Tommy still talking and paying no attention to him. He stuck his finger into the pail. The milk felt warm. Pulling his finger out, he put it into his mouth and tasted the warm sweet, creamy flavor of fresh milk. It seemed thick to him and reminded him of butter.

This is the real stuff, he thought. No plastic containers from the store here. This is neat!

Gus patted the side of Maw who was still munching on her food. She turned around and looked wide-eyed at Gus, as if giving her approval.

"Hey," called Gus to Addie. "What do I do now?"

Tommy and Addie came over to admire the pail full of milk and Addie picked it up and looked it over. "Not much hair, not much dirt. Looks like a first-rate job to me. What ya think, Tommy?"

Tommy patted Gus on the back and helped him carry the pail of milk to the barn entrance. "Now don't be sloshin' the milk on the way to the cookshack, boy," he instructed.

While Addie hurried ahead, Gus struggled with both his hands to carry the pail back to the cookshack. Wait until Mom hears I milked a cow, thought Gus. She won't believe it.

Just then another thought interrupted Gus's pride in his new accomplishment. A frown crossed his face. Just when was he going to see his mother again?

When Gus entered the cookshack with the milk he saw a big pile of wood that Alex had chopped. It was neatly piled up alongside the stove and pushed back out of the way. On top of the stove his pot of potatoes was cooking along with pots of boiling soup and stew. There was enough food to feed an army, Gus decided, but that was really what these men were—an army of lumberjacks.

Addie, waiting for Gus's milk, took and poured it into another pail which had a piece of cloth over it. Then she moved the cloth over the first pail and poured the milk back into it. She did this several times. "This is to strain the hair and dirt out of the milk," she explained to Gus. "I'm gonna cover this and set it on the back porch to cool. Ta-marrow morning after the cream raises off it, I'll make butter from the cream."

Suddenly Gus felt proud that he was able to contribute to the work in the cookshack. He turned just in time to get hit in the face with his flour bag apron. It was Alex. "Come on, we got work to do," he insisted.

The boys lugged big pots and bowls of food and poured pitchers of piping hot coffee. There was beef stew that had been bubbling on the back of the stove most of the day. There was also Gus's boiled potatoes, canned tomatoes, bread and butter, and huge wedges of pie.

As soon as the food was on the table, Alex went out the back door and struck a large iron triangle with a hammer, calling the men to eat.

Standing aside, Gus counted fifty-six men as they rushed past him for their places at the tables. Within a few minutes the plates that were heaping with food were almost bare and the men were on their way to the bunkhouse.

Gus and Alex worked side by side, stuffing themselves with leftovers as they washed, rinsed, and dried the dishes. After dishes were done, the places set for breakfast, and the floor swept, Gus went to the kitchen to see if Addie needed any more help.

Addie was getting the big pots and pans set for the next day's meals. "Ya look like ya can use some sleep, boy. Why don't ya go join Tommy and the rest of the men in the bunkhouse? It's time to call it a day."

Gus was glad to hear that. It had been a long hard day. His feet hurt in his big heavy boots; his hands hurt from peeling potatoes and milking the cow; and his stomach hurt from eating too many leftovers.

Gus left the cookshack and crossed the yard to the bunkhouse. It was dark outside, and the cold crisp air seemed to hold the promise of snow.

Chapter 8
A Greenhorn's Welcome

The lamps in the bunkhouse sent a warm glow across the yard, but Gus felt everything but warm and comfortable as he stepped into the crude building where he would spend the night. Glancing across the room he saw some of the men in their long underwear lying in their bunks. Others were sitting on the benches talking, and a few were huddled around the stoves playing checkers.

Gus could not believe the horrible smell. Haven't these guys ever heard of using deodorant? he wondered. Adding to the odor of unshowered lumberjacks were racks full of wet mittens and socks, steaming above the stoves. What a sight, thought Gus. What a smell! I bet Mr. Kristie at school would really think this was great—a real bunkhouse!

Gus made his way through the men to the bunk Tommy had assigned him. He was hoping Tommy would already be there, so he would know someone.

Just then Gus heard a friendly voice among the lumberjacks. It was Tommy. He was standing in his long red underwear, talking with some men at the rear of the bunkhouse.

"There ya are, boy. Did ya remember to bring in swamp grass for your bunk like I told ya?"

Gus scrunched his face. He had been so busy all day that he had forgotten.

"No matter," Tommy continued. "I got ya some **hay feathers** and got your bunk set up. When you're ready, strip to your skinnies and roll in."

Gus was grateful for Tommy's friendship. It was good to know he'd be in the bunk below. The idea of going to sleep in a room full of strangers had been bothering Gus.

Gus looked around at the faces of the men.

"Let me do some introductions," said Tommy. "Boys," he called out in a loud voice. "I want ya to meet Gus, the boy from the slashin' fire. Some of ya might have had an introduction to him this mornin' at breakfast."

Gus could hear the men grumble in response to the last comment.

"Gus here is lendin a hand in the cookshack. He's the new **crumb-chaser**." Gus saw that some of the men continued what they were doing, as if Tommy had said nothing to them.

One old man, who was playing checkers and had a lean, hawk-like face, gave Gus a smile that seemed to curl his mustache. "Welcome, **greenhorn**. I'm Moonshine Jay!" The men around the checker table all nodded their heads in welcome and then went back to their game.

A 'jack with two weeks growth of whiskers on his face and breath so bad it could melt a candle, came up and introduced himself. "Boy," he said, "I'm Rat-hole Andy, the meanest, whiskey-fightin' man in the camp—the most independent man on earth.

"There ain't no law that can touch me. Not even smallpox can catch me. I don't fear any man, beast, or even the devil. It's a pleasure to make your acquaintance, boy. But I warn ya, I don't like no **buckwheaters**."

Gus swallowed hard and smiled, "Pleased to make your acquaintance, sir."

"Hey, the boy's got manners! I like that in a boy." Andy smiled at Gus. Half of the lumberjack's teeth were missing and the other half were rotten and covered with dirty, brown juice. Gus wanted to turn away but knew he had better not.

For a time Gus was saved from Rat Hole Andy by Tommy's introductions of other lumberjacks. He met Cousin Jack, the Cornish Cussin' Man, Choppin' Charlie, and many others. Gus knew he would never remember their names by morning.

"Hey Tommy," called Rat-hole Andy. "Have ya taught the boy the Lumberjack Commandments yet?"

Tommy looked up at Andy and gave him a dirty look. "Ah, leave the boy alone. He's worked hard ta-day. He's tired."

Andy got real close to Gus's face. This *is* the meanest, whiskey-fighting man in camp, thought Gus. He stood still as Andy crinkled up one eye and smiled a big, smelly grin right into Gus's face.

"Tommy," he said as brown juice oozed out around his mouth. "Let me ask the boy if he would like to learn the Commandments."

Gus was sure by now that he had no choice. Andy looked mean, and he smelled worse.

"Yes, sir. I would like to learn the Commandments."

"See, Tommy. Ya got a polite boy here."

Just then Ol' Moonshine Jay stood, pushing his chair back from his checker game. "Bein' I'm the oldest 'jack and the orneriest 'jack in this here neck of the woods, Andy, don't ya suppose it's my job to teach this here greenhorn the Commandments?" Moonshine Jay stared a mean, insistent look at Andy.

"Ya know there, ol' man, ya'r probably right on both counts," said Andy, and he stood aside for Moonshine to be seen clearly.

The old man pulled on his suspenders. Then, he licked his fingers and curled the ends of his mustache with spit. In a loud, deep voice he said,"Repeat after me!

"Thou shalt not make to thyself any comforts.

"Thou shalt not take thy boss's name in vain.

"You will work from before sunup to after sundown, six days a week and be glad to have a job.

"Thou shalt always speak well of your brother 'jacks.

"And you will never kiss another 'jack's girl—that is, of course, without his permission.

"Ya got all that boy? Now repeat it!"

Gus got it. It was kind of a joke, making fun of working in a lumber camp. With only a little help from Tommy, Gus repeated the words that Moonshine had spoken. When he finished, all the men clapped and patted Gus on the back.

"There ya go, boy. You're a real 'jack now," said Moonshine. "And in celebration, here, have a pinch of **snoose**." Moonshine reached deep into his dirty pants pocket and pulled out some brown, flaky stuff. "Here, have a chew on me."

At first, Gus thought he was kidding and shook his head no.

Tommy elbowed Gus in the ribs. "Ya can't turn him down, boy. This ol' man runs the bunkhouse. Ya got to take it out of respect. It's only chewin' tobacca," whispered Tommy.

Gus walked over and held his hand out to old Moonshine as he dropped a pinch of the stuff into his hand.

"Hey fellas," called Andy, "I don't think this here boy has ever chewed before." The men all stared in surprise at Gus.

"There's nothin' to it," Andy continued. Just put a wad in the side of your lip and when ya work up a spit, let it fling."

Gus wrinkled his face and took a pinch between his fingers. He turned to Tommy. "I can't do this," he whispered. "If my mom knew she would ground me for life!"

Just then Andy interrupted. "If ya don't like this kind, boy, there's plenty others ta try."

"Hey Andy," said Tommy, "why don't ya tell the boy the tale of chewin' while he tries his first dip."

Gus gave Tommy a dirty look. But Tommy only winked as he tried to turn everyone's attention away from Gus.

"Yeah, Andy," said Gus, who now understood Tommy's plan. "Tell me the story about chewin'. And if I don't like this kind, then maybe I'll try the others.

"That's the spirit, boy," growled Moonshine as he stood to spit the brown tobacco juice into a can beside the checkerboard and then sat down.

Gus could tell Andy liked to hear himself talk, and knew the story could take a while. Gus dropped some of the chew onto the floor and put his foot on it to cover it up.

"Well, the story goes like this," began Andy. "Only sissies smoke cigarettes, or pimp sticks, and only bosses smoke cigars. So that leaves tobacca chewin' to us 'jacks. Now there are several types of tobacca, like Spearhead, Battle Axe, Five Brothers, and Peerless. Ya chew these 'til the flavor is all gone and then ya take it out and lay it somewhere to dry. After it's all dried out like, ya smoke it in your pipe.

"Like ol' Moonshine does, right after his grub in the evenin'. Right, Moonshine?"

"That's right, Andy," responded Moonshine.

"Ya know, after ya smoke yar pipe, ya can take the ashes and put them in your boots ta cut down on the foot stink. That's why all our wet socks in here smell so good when they're drying—like tobacca chew."

Gus looked at Tommy and swallowed hard.

"Why, I've been in some camps where ya have ta sleep outside cause the steamin' socks smell so bad over the fire. But not ours. Right, boys?"

The men all nodded their heads with satisfaction.

"After ya smoke yar pipe, the stash you don't use for your socks ya can scrape out and get yarself **Swedish brain powder**. Now that will give you a lift clear through the trees."

Moonshine called out, "Tell 'im about **Scandahoovian dynamite**."

"I was gettin' ta that, ol' man. Don't get yar suspenders in a knot," said Andy.

"Scandahoovian Dynamite is the tar ball left in yar pipe. Ya chew that—it's nasty stuff—and it'll turn yar insides green, it will.

"Ain't that right, boys?" The men all chimed in to agree.

While everyone was agreeing with everyone else, Gus dropped more of the chewing tobacco, grinding it into the dirty floor boards with his boot.

Andy strolled over to the potbelly stove where Moonshine was playing checkers. "Come over here to the **amen corner**, boy. I want ya ta see how ta do this."

Gus followed Andy to the stove and watched. Andy leaned over the stove and with his hands on his hips spit a long stream of brown juice onto the hot stove top. "Thar ya have it, boy, the best darn air cleaner in the world, and it kills germs ta boot.

"Take a deep breath of that, boy. It'll clean yar head out every time."

Everyone looked at Gus as he breathed deeply, trying hard not to get sick from the added smell of tobacco juice on a hot stove.

The men all smiled as Gus managed a grin. "That smells . . . . Really. Really, it does."

The men all stood wide-eyed as they watched Gus. Gus knew he'd better not say anything more. He also knew he wasn't going to get away with not trying the chewing tobacco.

"Well, boy, pop it inta yar mouth and tell us what ya think." Everyone, even ol' Moonshine, watched closely.

Gus turned to Tommy who whispered, "Ya gonna have to do it. Just ball it up and hold it in your mouth for a second. Ya can spit it out as soon as they aren't lookin'."

Fearful what the 'jacks would do if he didn't try, and fearful what his mother would do if he did try, Gus shuddered. Then he took the tiny pinch between his fingers, pulled back his lip, and dropped the tobacco in his mouth.

Mom's gonna be so mad, he thought for a second. And then he began to taste the burn in his mouth. At first he decided it was just hot. Then it got real bitter, and his tongue began to burn.

"You're workin' up a spit, boy," howled Andy as he grinned and showed his dirty, brown teeth. "Give the boy a spit pail," he called.

Everyone's eyes were on Gus. His stomach started to rumble. When the spit pail was passed he looked into it and saw the vilest, nastiest pail of spit he could have ever imagined.

"I'm gonna be sick," Gus yelled as he ran out the door of the bunkhouse.

All the men hooted and howled at Gus and laughed as hard as they could.

"He's no greenhorn no more," called Moonshine as he went back to his checker game, quite satisfied with all that had happened. "He's just green."

When Gus returned, he didn't want to look at anyone. He just wanted to go to bed. Crawling up into the top bunk, he took off his boots, jeans, and shirt. Leaving on his long johns, he settled into the bunk.

Gus could hear the men talking and laughing about him, but he didn't care. At least he didn't have brown, rotted teeth like theirs.

Gus had just lain down when he heard a clanging sound. Oh no, it can't be time to get up, he thought. I haven't even gone to bed yet.

"**Douse the glim**! Lights out!" called a man's voice.

It must be the Big Push, thought Gus, since he and Alex were the only men that didn't bunk with the rest of them.

All around the bunkhouse kerosene lamps went out and men wrestled with their clothes, skinning down to their long johns in the dark.

When everything was quiet someone at the far end called out, "Did someone let Betty in?"

"I don't know what fer," was the response. "She won't catch us no bugs."

"No, but she kills the rats that bring 'um."

Rats? Bugs? In the bunkhouse? wondered Gus.

Chapter 9
A Lousy Night!

Gus rolled over in his wooden bunk. The hay which was supposed to make the bunk more comfortable lay flat and scratchy under his heavy blanket. This is supposed to make sleeping easier? Gus wondered to himself.

Gus could hear someone walk past the bunks and open the door. "Tarnation, Betty, get yourself in here!" called a voice, and the door squeaked shut again.

Hardly had Gus begun to settle down again when he heard some of the men snoring. "Oh no, I can't believe this," he thought out loud. Rolling over again, he pulled the blanket up over his head and tucked it around his chin. There, he thought, maybe I won't hear all those men sawing logs in their sleep.

Warm and tired, Gus began to drift off to sleep. Then he felt something like a needle prick him on the face. Sitting up quickly he rubbed his face. Then he felt another sharp prick. This time it was on his arm, not just once, but twice.

In the darkness of the bunkhouse, Gus whispered down to Tommy. "Tommy, there's something in my bed biting me. I can't see what it is."

"Be quiet, boy. It's just the bedbugs," was Tommy's reply. "Y'ar sleepin' in a **cootie cage**. What do ya expect?"

"Bedbugs? Cootie cage?" exclaimed Gus. "Let me out of here!" Gus scrambled around the wooden bunk, feeling for his clothes.

A voice that sounded like Moonshine called out. "Bedbugs, boy. Get used to 'em. They're a fact of camp life. If ya listen careful, ya can hear the crawlers all around you. They kind of make a poppin' sound."

Gus sat up in the corner of his bunk with the blanket pulled over his head. How can they live like this? he wondered.

Another voice joined in the conversation. "Lice, **greybacks**, **pants rabbits**. They cling to every seam in your clothes. Ya can't get rid of 'em, boy. Ya'll be **crummy** with 'em ta-marrow.

"I've tried washin' 'em out, pickin' 'em out. I heard the best way to get a couple hours sleep is to get up, take off your long johns and reverse 'em. It takes them pants rabbits about two hours to crawl through to the other side and get a taste of yar skin again."

Tommy reached up and gave the bottom of Gus's bunk a kick. "See what ya started now."

A third voice chimed in from the other side of the bunkhouse. Gus knew it was Rat-hole Andy.

"Hey boy, maybe this'll work. Ta-marrow when y'ar in the cookshack, sneak some salt and pour it into your long johns. Rub it all over and do it right before ya go to bed.

"In the mornin' go down by the stream and strip out of your clothes. I've heard it told that those greybacks jump right outta your clothes inta the water. Ya see, they're so thirsty from chewin' on your salty hide, they jump inta the water for a drink. And if ya move fast enough, ya can get your britches back on before they catch ya."

The men in the bunkhouse laughed and hooted.

'That's a good one, Rat-hole," they called.

"All right, ya hooligans," said Tommy. "We got a long day ahead of us. We better get our rest."

Rat-hole called out again. "Hey, boy, if ya catch some good ones, I'll race 'em with mine ta-marrow on the hot stove."

Gus was more tired and miserable than he had ever been in his entire life. His stomach still rumbled from the chew, and now his bed was full of bugs. How was he ever going to get to sleep? He longed to be home in his waterbed.

At four in the morning, just after Gus had finally fallen asleep, Tommy booted the bottom of Gus's bunk. "Ya better get up before Addie comes to get ya. Didn't ya hear the first bell?"

Gus hadn't heard the first bell, and he wished he hadn't heard Tommy. Feeling around his miserable bunk, he found his clothes. As he put his shirt on, his arms began to itch. When he pulled on his pants, his legs began to itch. He scratched his arms and legs, and the more he scratched the bug bites, the more he itched.

As he rubbed his legs and arms, Gus looked around him. Small kerosene lamps were lit throughout the bunkhouse casting weird shapes on the floor and bunks. A few men who had to get up early or go to the outhouse were talking.

In the dim light, Gus could see a man in long, red underwear standing in the corner in front of some wash buckets. He was dunking his head up and down in the water and rubbing his stubbly whiskers.

Turning to Gus he said, "Boy, ya better wash up a bit before ya see Miss Addie, or she'll throw you in the tub with the dirty dishes and scrub you with a wire brush."

Running his hand over his face, Gus could feel the swollen bug bites. Maybe it would be a good idea to wash, he thought.

As the man moved aside, Gus could see it was Rat-hole Andy. "Here, boy. Wash here. I'm finished."

In the dim light Gus tried to look into the bucket to see if the water was still clean.

"It's clean, boy, and hot ta boot. I just got it off the stove. I only dunked my head and rinsed my mouth."

The thought of washing in the same water as Andy turned Gus's stomach. But once again, he knew he had no choice. He scooped up a handful of hot water and rubbed it over his face.

"Ain't ya gonna rinse your mouth, boy?"

Gus shook his head, "No, I don't think so. Thanks anyway."

"Well, don't go talkin' ta me ta-day if ya don't rinse your mouth."

Gus snickered at the thought of that dirty man with half his teeth rotted being worried about washing and rinsing his mouth. Then he shook the water off his face and made his way across the room to the door.

Gus was near the door when he heard a loud meow followed by a great hiss. Betty arched her back and spit wildly at him, all the while flinging her tail back and forth. I must have stepped on her tail, Gus thought.

Stepping back in the darkness to see where the cat had gone, he stumbled over the spit bucket, which had made him ill the night before. It rolled across the bunkhouse floor, spilling its contents and leaving a dirty, wet trail. Jumping back to get out of the mess, Gus knocked over a chair.

"Quiet!" a rough voice called out.

Gus stood silently for a second and held his breath. Just then Betty rubbed up against his leg.

Gus reached down to make peace with the three-legged animal. Betty grabbed his hand with her claws, biting hard into his thumb. Gus jerked back his hand as the cat ran off into the shadows of the bunkhouse.

Gus squeezed his thumb and gritted his teeth so as not to yell out in pain.

That stinking cat, this stinking bunkhouse, this rotten lumber camp. I want to go home! thought Gus. If only I knew how I got here, I'd be able to get back home, back to school, or even back to fight with Al.

Standing for a second in the dim stillness, Gus got himself together and opened the squeaky bunkhouse door. Outside it was still dark, but from the reflection of the moon Gus could see snow gently falling.

I've got to get back home. I can't live like this, thought Gus as he rubbed the welts on his face and arms.

Gus cut across the yard to the cookshack. He could see the light from the lamps, already lit.

As Gus entered the warm room, Alex was stacking wood beside the cook stove. Alex looked up, spotted the welts on Gus's face, and broke into a grin.

"You look like you slept with the lice brigade," he laughed.

Just then Addie entered the kitchen from the dining hall. She took one look at Gus and knew what kind of night he had had.

"Ya be mindin' your mouth, Alex. Here, Gus, take the lantern and pail and go milk Maw. She'll be ready for ya."

Gus picked up the milk pail and the lantern and left the kitchen, glad not to have to work with Alex for a while.

Catching Maw for milking was not easy, but Gus finally got her to the manger where he tied her up. Chasing a cow around the barnyard was fun in its own way, Gus decided, and much better than working with Alex!

Gus had just finished milking when Tommy came in to feed the horses. He leaned over the manger and looked down at the boy. "Ya had a poor night, didn't ya boy? I know how they are 'cause I've had my share of them, too. The longer y'ar in camp, the less the bugs bother ya. The skin doesn't bump up like that so much either.

"Why most of us 'jacks just take it as part of camp life, like the snow and ice and the good cookin' of a pretty woman by the name of Addie."

Gus looked up from his milking and smiled at Tommy, whose eyes were bright and twinkling.

Just then, Gus felt something rub up against his leg. He knew what that was. It was mean, three-legged Betty!

"I heard the ruckus in the bunkhouse with the cat this morning. As soon as ya make peace with that critter, the better off ya'll be, boy."

Gus turned around to see the cat sitting wobbly-like, waiting for her morning cream.

He squirted milk at her, and she lapped it off her face and around her mouth.

Both he and Tommy laughed at the crazy cat.

Chapter 10
The Fight

In the cookshack Gus strained the milk and put it outside to cool. He noticed yesterday's milk had a thick layer of cream that had risen to the top during the night.

"Addie," he called, "do you want me to bring in the milk from yesterday to make butter?"

"Does it look like I got four hands, boy? I'm busy. Butter-makin' is work ya do when ya are done with your work."

Gus scratched at the bug bites on his face. I guess that was the wrong thing to ask this morning, he thought.

"As long as you're out there," Addie called, "bring in wood from the pile behind the shack. When you're done, go put the long sweetenin' out and get the tables ready for the men.

"Alex, get yourself in here," she continued. "I'm runnin' behind. I need ya' to make some **flappers**."

Gus ran and grabbed an armload of wood from a big pile behind the cookshack and carried it into the kitchen.

"Gus, throw a couple of logs into the **baker**. I need to get the fire hotter so I can put the griddle on."

Gus looked at the stove and wondered where he was supposed to put the wood. It was the strangest looking stove he had ever seen. Besides, he had never really watched Alex closely enough to know how to stoke the fire.

Addie watched Gus hesitate and then came around to the stove. As she threw open a door near the bottom, Gus could see a bed of coals already glowing red. "Put it in, boy, and hurry it up. Don't want to lose my heat."

Gus dropped a couple of small logs into the fire. Sparks began to fly up toward the door as Addie slammed it shut. That wasn't so bad, he thought.

Gus had just finished stacking the rest of the wood beside the stove when he heard Addie and Alex arguing.

"Yeah, well, you're the cook around here. Why don't ya do your own job?"

"Well, ya are the cook's helper, boy, and if I tell ya to follow the recipe for flappers, then that's what I mean."

Gus could see Alex had made a big mess at the cook's table, with flour all over the place. There was also a big bowl piled high with flour and eggs.

"I told ya to make flappers, not a mess. Look now, ya wasted all these **cakleberries**. All ya had to do was follow the words in the book."

Addie looked down at the big brown cookbook with its stained pages. "Ya ain't even got it turned to the right page."

"Well, if you weren't such a terrible cook, I wouldn't have to be doing your job. I'm gonna tell my pa to make you take the **long walk** out of camp," yelled Alex.

"She's not a terrible cook," Gus yelled back, "and you're a troublemaker. Any idiot can read a recipe," Gus glared at Alex.

Suddenly a look of knowing came across Addie's face. "Alex, can ya read, boy?"

"You don't need no book learnin' to work in a lumber camp. I bet dummy here can't read either," insisted Alex as he stared angrily at Gus.

"I can read. I read really well. I like to read. I thought everyone knew how to read," said Gus in a serious tone.

Alex was angrier than ever. He stormed out of the kitchen into the dining hall, letting the door swing shut behind him.

"Gus, if ya can really read, boy, clean up this mess and stir me up some flappers from the recipe. I'm runnin' behind and need your help. Alex can finish settin' the tables for the men."

There was no time for more arguments. Alex stomped in and out of the kitchen several times, getting dishes to put on the tables. Gus cleaned up the mess and found the pancake recipe. He made a huge batch for Addie to bake on the griddle. Soon she had a stack of flappers a yard high waiting to be served.

As soon as everything was ready Addie rang the triangle and the men filed into the hall. Taking their places at the tables, they ate quietly, talking only when they asked for the long sweetening, black lead, or more food. Alex and Gus poured mugs full of black lead, refilled the dishes of maple syrup, and brought out stacks of flappers.

At first it started as a low rumbling throughout the dining hall. Finally one man stood up and spit out a mouthful of coffee on the floor. Then he grabbed the man that sat next to him, picking him up by the shirt collar and shaking him with all his might.

"Ya din-dang polecat! What ya doin' givin' me salt for my sweetenin'?"

The man being jerked gathered his senses and grabbed the other 'jack by the neck. He squeezed so hard that Gus thought the other 'jack's eyes were going to pop out of his head.

Then another 'jack stood up and threw his coffee from his mug. "He got me too!"

Men all over the room began grabbing at the men who sat next to them, and the fight was on. There was pushing and shoving and toe-to-toe slugging. Tin dishes flew in every direction!

Gus backed against the wall as he watched two men tackle a large 'jack. The three rolled against a table leg and tipped over the table. Rat-hole Andy, not to be left out of the fun, was in on it, too. Gus watched as he tackled a 'jack twice his size from behind and then jumped on his back and chewed on his ear.

Addie, hearing the commotion, ran out of the kitchen, banging on a large frying pan with a wooden spoon. "STOP!" she yelled as loudly as she could.

By this time Tommy ran out the door with a group of men who knew better than to get into the fight.

Gus watched as Addie ran back into the kitchen and returned with a shotgun. Aiming it toward the ceiling, she shot off a blast. A grey cloud formed above her head, and the smell of gunpowder filled the air.

The men stopped and looked at Addie, who held the shotgun out in front of her.

Just then Tommy returned with the Big Push. "What in tar-nation is going on in here?" he bellowed. "Can't you men eat in peace and not act like a band of hooligans?"

"Addie," he said, "put that blasted gun away before someone gets hurt!" Addie went into the kitchen and quickly returned without the gun.

"Now who started this?" demanded the Push.

One man who was covered with maple syrup spoke from the back of the room. His eyes were red and swollen. "I guess, boss . . .," he said, "I did. This rascal beside me loaded my black lead with salt instead of sweetenin'."

Another man in worse shape than the first stood up. "He did it ta me too!"

Other men stepped forward from around the room and said their coffee was full of salt. The Push ordered Addie to bring in the coffee pot. He picked up a mug from the floor, wiped it out on the bottom of his vest, and poured himself a mug of coffee.

"T'ain't nothin' wrong with this here black lead." Going over to a table that hadn't been cleared off or tipped over, he poured sugar into the mug.

Taking a big gulp, he pulled back the mug and spit out the coffee. "Addie, I want ya to taste this and tell me who's responsible for putting salt in the sugar bowls?"

Addie sheepishly took the mug from the Push and took a sip. The coffee was so full of salt that it bit at her tongue.

Alex, who had been hiding in the kitchen, peeked out from behind the kitchen door. "It's Gus's fault. It's his job to set the tables and put out the sweetenin'."

The men all started to stir. "Where's that boy?" they demanded.

"I didn't do it," cried Gus. "Tell them, Addie. Tell them how I was helping you in the kitchen this morning."

The 'jacks filed out of the dining hall, wiping food from their clothes and giving Gus dirty looks as they passed by.

As Rat-hole Andy passed he gave a low, deep, animal-like growl.

"I didn't do it, Andy, honest. It wasn't me."

"Sir," said Addie to the Push, "I don't know how the salt got in the sweetenin' bowls, but this here boy was helpin' me in the kitchen this mornin'. Wasn't he, Alex?"

"I don't care how this happened. I just want this mess cleaned up and this boy out of my camp!"

"My apologies, sir," interrupted Tommy, "but could the boy work till the end of the week?"

"Why? So he can catch a nice ride to the next settlement? You want me to make this easy on him after this mess?"

"Well, sir, it's not just that. Ya see I signed my name to his credit slip at the company store. If he finishes out the week, at least it will take care of paying up his expenses here."

"I really didn't do this..." protested Gus. "It had to have been Alex."

"Hush, boy," said Addie.

"This is so unfair. I didn't do anything," insisted Gus.

"Alex," shouted the Push. "Where'd ya go, boy?"

The Push leaned down low and stared into Gus's face, wagging his finger back and forth. "I'll let you work the week out to help Tommy here with the bill. But the next wagon out of here, I want you on. Understand?"

Gus nodded his head.

"Alex!" bellowed the Push as he left the dining hall.

"I'm sorry, boy," said Addie. "I know ya wouldn't do something like that."

Gus jammed his hands deep into his pockets and hung his head. "It's not fair, it's just not fair," he said over and over as tears came to his eyes.

"Lots of things in life aren't fair, boy," said Tommy. "You just seem to be on the receivin' end more than most of us." Tommy reached out and patted Gus on the back. Gus pulled away. "Why didn't ya make the boss listen?"

Tommy put his arm around him. "That man doesn't listen to anyone. It's best to wait 'til he cools down and then maybe we can talk to him."

Gus, angry at the whole situation, pulled away from Tommy.

"Why don't ya go out and cool down a bit, yourself?" said Tommy as he reached down and picked up a pancake that lay on the floor. "Here, give Napoleon a bite to eat. I bet he's hungry. I'll give Addie a hand 'til ya get back."

Gus looked up at Tommy. He knew Tommy was right. That jerk Al, or Alex, had done it to him again. Taking the pancake from Tommy, Gus went outside.

Some of the men were still standing around by the bunkhouse talking. Several had swollen eyes, already starting to turn black and blue. How was he ever going to be able to face them tonight? Gus wondered. I want to go home, now! he thought as the tears ran down his face.

Gus slowly walked over to where Napoleon was chained. The bear called out with a howl for the food in Gus's hand. Gus tore off pieces of the pancake and gingerly fed it to him.

When the pancake was gone, the bear licked the syrup off Gus's hands. Gus started feeling better. He sat down on the ground and the bear playfully lay beside him, rolling over on its back in hopes of getting its belly scratched.

Gus smiled at the bear. Napoleon wasn't really a cub anymore. He was more like a teenager, almost as big as an adult but still playful and in need of attention.

Gus rubbed the bear as it slapped at his hands and licked at his sticky fingers with his long, pink tongue.

Gus was just starting to forget his troubles when he heard a low, deep growl coming from the nearby trees. Napoleon quickly rose to his feet and sniffed the air, pulling hard against his chain toward the woods.

Gus jumped to his feet and stood listening. I wonder if that's Rat-hole trying to get even? he thought.

Gus remained quiet. Then he heard it again. That was no human, thought Gus. That's the cougar! He ran across the yard to the dining hall. Throwing the door open, he nearly knocked down Tommy who was on his way out.

"Tommy! Come quick. The cougar is out there!" yelled Gus excitedly. "Will Napoleon be all right? The cougar is in the woods right beside Napoleon. Will the cougar go after him?"

"Ya don't know much about bears, do ya?" said Tommy who seemed more concerned with Gus's lack of knowledge about the woods than the presence of a cougar. "The only natural enemy of a cougar is the bear. A cougar won't bother a bear unless it's a tiny cub and the cougar is starvin'. Don't go worryin' about Napoleon. He'll be fine.

"But you watch out for yourself. Stay out of the woods and stick close to camp.

"Now I want ya to help Miss Addie with this mess, and I'll go take a look for that cat. At noon, ya'll go with me to deliver dinners. I heard Alex has taken off for a bit, and I don't know if he'll be back for dinnerin' out. Maybe we can come up with something that will change the boss's mind about ya."

Gus smiled at Tommy. Tommy really was his friend and was trying to help.

"All right, Tommy, I'll see ya later," said Gus. He entered the dining hall and started helping Addie put things back in order.

Chapter 11
A Thing or Two

The mess in the dining hall seemed to take forever to clean up. It didn't help when Addie had to leave to pull dinners together for the cutting crew.

After the last pancake was unstuck from the wall and the last tin mug was found outdoors, Gus went into the kitchen to see if Alex had returned. Gus couldn't see him anywhere. He knew Addie would need his help getting the baskets and boxes filled and into the wagon.

Gus helped Addie as they stirred the pots of stew, piled loaves of bread into baskets, and packed cans of tomatoes into boxes. They were just about finished when Addie mentioned that she could hear the clanking of Tommy's wagon coming up from the barn.

"Ya better start gettin' the baskets around and pile the boxes by the door. Tommy will be needin' your help out there ta-day."

Gus was glad. After this morning, he needed a chance to get away for a while.

Tommy pulled Dick and Jim around by the backdoor of the cookshack and Gus started loading the baskets and boxes onto the wagon.

"Hold up there, boy," called Tommy. "Taday Addie generally makes stew for the men. The stew pots have to go in first. Then we pack the boxes and baskets around it, to keep it warm and hold 'em steady.

"Come here and take hold of the reins. Talk real sweet to Dick and Jim, and they'll hold real still for ya. I'll go help Addie with the big pots."

Tommy disappeared into the cookshack and soon returned carrying a huge, steaming pot of stew.

"How's me boys doin' for ya, Gus? asked Tommy.

"They're fine, just fine," Gus said as he looked up at the big horses and reached out to give Jim a pat. Dick, who was getting restless started pawing at the ground with his hoof.

"Steady, boy, steady. It's all right. Tommy will be right back," said Gus gently as he held tight to the reins.

Tommy, who had gone back into the cookshack returned with a second pot of stew and slid it up onto the wagon bed.

"There ya go, boy," said Tommy as he came around the wagon, taking the reins from Gus's hands. "Ya work well with horses, boy, and they seem to like ya just fine. Maybe I could get the Push to allow ya to come work with me away from Alex."

"Oh, is that right?" came a booming voice from around the other side of the wagon. It was the Push.

"I thought this here boy was supposed to be leaving camp at the end of the week, Tommy?

"Ya know, boy," said the Push to Gus, "I've been thinking. Since your friend Tommy here is so concerned about you paying your bill back at the company store, I thought I would help him out by givin' you another job to do. This way, it will help ya pay your credit up even quicker.

"Tonight before you hit the bunk, I want you to black grease my good boots. Alex's, too. Ya know, when ya pay a lot of money for somethin' like good-fittin' boots, ya should take care of 'em. My boots need a thorough goin' over and so do Alex's. Before you hit the hay tonight, I want the job done."

Gus's face reddened, and he bit down hard on his lip to try to keep from saying anything.

"You got a problem with that, boy?" asked the Push.

"No sir," replied Gus.

"Good, good. I'll make sure ya get the boots when ya finished in the cookshack ta-night. Ya know, I think this was one of Alex's better ideas. That boy is bound to make a great Push someday," he said with pride.

Tommy knew better than to say anything, and he gave Gus a look to keep quiet too.

"By the way, Tommy, I ran across Alex and he said he would be here to make the dinner run with you. So make sure ya wait for the boy."

"Oh?" said Tommy, "I thought I would take Gus since he is right here. And besides Alex should get out of camp a bit 'til the men cool down."

"You want to take Gus out into those woods with all those hungry 'jacks that couldn't finish their breakfasts this mornin' because of him? I don't think that's a good idea, Tommy. You just wait up for Alex."

Gus stood staring. I don't believe this, he thought. Alex caused all the trouble and I get all the blame!

Just then, Alex came sauntering across the yard with a smug look on his face. "Hey Gus, did I tell ya your flappers went over great this mornin'? Ya read recipes real good."

Gus was so mad, he could have punched Alex right then and there. But Gus now understood why Alex put salt in the sugar bowls. He was getting back at him because he could read.

Addie came out of the cookshack door and called to the men, "Tommy, ya better be goin'. It's gettin' late."

Alex jumped on the back of the wagon and Addie gave him a dirty look. "I thought ya probably applied for a job as the boss since doin' proper kitchen work is too hard for ya."

"Addie," snapped the Push, "Ya best tend to your own knittin' or you'll be cookin' elsewhere."

Gus pushed past Addie into the kitchen. He opened the stove door, and dropped in a fresh log, watching the sparks fly up and dance in the air.

"It's not fair, boy, that ya get the dirty end of the stick all the time 'cause of that poorly bred young'un," said Addie.

"Ya are a good boy, Gus, and don't ya go forgettin' it. That boy will get his due someday, and the price he pays will be high."

Gus looked at Addie. He knew she liked him and was on his side, and that was what really mattered.

Gus helped serve lunch to the few men that stayed in camp. Some refused to take black lead from Gus and others commented, "I hope you're not plannin' on sleepin' in the bunkhouse this night, boy."

When suppertime came, Addie had Gus work in the kitchen, putting food into bowls, slicing bread, and cutting pies. She had Alex serve the coffee and work the dining room. Addie understood that it wouldn't take much for the men to explode into another fight and if that happened, maybe this time it would mean her job, too.

After supper Gus and Alex washed the dishes together but never said a word to each other. When they finished, Alex sat down and pulled off his stinky boots and handed them to Gus.

"These are for you. Pa's boots are over by the door with a tin of boot grease. There's writin' on the side of the tin. I'm sure you can read how to grease 'em up just right," Alex gave Gus a rat grin.

Gus wanted to shove the boots in Alex's face.

"Excuse me, boys," interrupted Addie, "the work is done in the kitchen. Gus, you better get yourself to the bunkhouse.

"Alex, I'm finished with ya also, so good night." Addie put her hands on her hips and stood watching as the boys left the dining hall in opposite directions, making sure the two of them didn't start a fight.

Gus carried the boots at arm's length because they smelled so bad. The tin of grease had an old rag wrapped around it, and it was filthy and smelly, too.

On his way to the bunkhouse, Gus walked the path to the outhouse. Looking out of the outhouse door to make sure no one was around, Gus dangled the boots over the two holes in the outhouse. It would serve them right, he laughed. Then he stopped himself, knowing he was already in enough trouble.

When Gus entered the bunkhouse, all the men were real quiet and stared at Gus.

Tommy came from the back of the room, put his arm around him, and escorted him through the men to his bunk.

The men started talking quietly among themselves and a fellow by the potbelly stove called out, "Hey, boys, I just got meself a new Paul Bunyan story. Published here in this gazette. Ya' wants me to read it to ya?"

Suddenly the room was full of noise and the men all chimed in, "All right, a new story!"

Gus smiled at the men, thinking about how excited they were to have a simple story read to them.

Gus sat down on the **deacon's bench** in front of the bunk and read the side of the grease tin on how to grease boots.

Most of the men gathered around the stove while the 'jack who was going to read sat in Moonshine's checker chair and prepared himself.

Even Rat-hole Andy flopped down beside the stove and made himself comfortable, pulling out a plug of tobacco and chewing while he made ready to listen.

Gus pried open the grease tin and began polishing the Push's boots with the old rag.

The man with the newspaper cleared his throat and began to read. "'Paul Bun-yan. Thar on--ce war a lumber camp. The near-est town were thir-thir-ty miles a-way.'

"Shucks, fellas, it sounds like us," the reader commented and all the men agreed.

"'The n-ear-est ni-bor are fox and b'ars who . . . who . . . who . . .', I don't know this word. It's spelled P-R-O-W-L."

"Prowl," said Gus, "the word is prowl."

The men all turned and stared at Gus as if they couldn't believe their ears.

Ol' Moonshine Jay, who was chewing on the end of his pipe spoke up, "Ya read, boy?"

"Sure, I read."

The lumberjacks all looked at one another and started to laugh.

"Ya read better than this here mangy excuse for a reader?" asked Moonshine.

"Yes, I read pretty well. I like to read." said Gus.

The men started talking among themselves and Rat-hole spoke up. "Hey boy, I'll grease the boss's boots for ya, if ya will read the story to us."

The men all thought that was a great idea. Rat-hole stood up and spit out a mouthful of juice into the spit can and took the newspaper from its owner. Without protest the owner handed the paper over. Everyone moved their chairs closer to Gus while Rat-hole took the grease and boots and sat on the floor waiting to hear the story.

"Paul Bunyan.

"Did you all know this is called an American folk tale? Actually, it's a tall tale. I learned that in school."

The men raised their eyebrows at the big words and nodded their heads at the boy's superior knowledge.

"'This is a lumber camp. The nearest town is thirty miles away. The nearest neighbors are the foxes and bears who prowl behind the cook shanty and the night owl, swooping swiftly across the face of the moon.'

"All they need to add is the growl of the cougar and Napoleon and this writer would be describing our camp," said Gus. The men sat listening, surprised at the great talent the boy possessed.

"'Over here is the bunkhouse. Inside, big, tired men sprawled across their bunks . . . .'"

Gus continued to read the whole story to the men, never missing a word or stumbling over a pronunciation.

"Boy," said Moonshine when Gus had finished. "Boy, I ain't never heard such sweet readin' in all my born days. Except, that is, when my dear ol' ma use ta read from the Good Book. Ma always would tell us young'uns how important it was to learn to read.

"Course we had no teachers around and Ma did her best with us boys. But Pa always needed us to work in the fields, clearin' land and there was always a stream full of fish waitin' to be caught.

"It's the only thing in my ol' age I ever regretted, not bein' able to read. So I could read the weekly gazette and the Good Book like Ma. "

Rat-hole stood up and showed Gus the great job he had done greasing the boots. "Ya know boy, this mornin' I could have chewed ya up and spit ya out for what ya done in the dinin' hall. But anyone that possesses a talent for readin' like you, can be forgiven for causin' trouble. Right, boys?"

The men agreed with Rat-hole.

"But I didn't do anything," insisted Gus. Then the men started to grumble among themselves again.

"It was Alex. He was mad 'cause I could read Addie's recipe book and he couldn't. He did it to get me in trouble and get me kicked out of camp!

"Ya got to believe me!"

The men listened with serious looks on their faces. "Ya, mean boy, ya are losin' your job 'cause that spoilt, good for nothin', pain in the . . . ."

"We get the picture, Rat-hole," interrupted Tommy. Tommy came over and stood beside Gus. The men listened carefully.

"There's not a thin' we can do about it, boys. The trouble's happened. The boss has put down the law and Gus will be leavin' camp on the next wagon out. It's best to leave things alone. We don't want the boy kicked out of camp before the wagon comes because of some silly prank, do we?"

The men agreed. "Tain't right, though, this here boy has to leave camp 'cause of that brat. That Alex should be taught a thing or two," said Andy.

Just then the metal triangle rang throughout the camp and the Push's voice echoed through the woods. "Nine o'clock, douse the glim! Lights out!"

Chapter 12
The Accident

The next morning when Gus arrived in the cookshack, the Push and Alex were already there, waiting for him.

"Well, boy, I see ya did a right fine job on the boots," said the Push in a nasty tone.

"Ah—thank you, sir," said Gus. "I hoped you would like what I did." After reading last night, Gus had forgotten all about the boots and was glad to hear Rat-hole had taken them to the Push's cabin.

"Are you tryin' to be smart-mouthed with me, boy?" bellowed the Push.

"Yeah, Pa, I think he's bein' smart-mouthed with ya. Aren't ya, boy?" said Alex as he pushed up against Gus and stared him right in the eyes.

Gus didn't know what was going on and stepped back.

"You tellin' me, boy, it weren't you that coated Alex's boots down with maple syrup and left 'em out for the bear to get at?"

"What are you talking about?" asked Gus.

"That there bear got a whiff of that syrup and broke loose of his chain and chewed Alex's boots up real good. Ya were smart not to have put my boots out to get chawed on, or I'd have your hide tanned and hung on the barn wall."

"But I . . . I didn't do it!"

"No, you don't do nothin' wrong, do ya? Nothin's ever your fault, is it, boy?

"I told ya to remember I was the Big Push around here, and I think you gone and forgot that."

"I didn't do it," interrupted Gus. "Rat-hole, he . . . . I read a story . . . and . . . ."

"Yeah boy, I think you're tellin' a story now. If Rat-hole got word that you were blaming him, he'd do worse to you than I'm gonna."

"But I . . . ."

"Boy, I want ya to finish the day out and after supper I want ya to take the long walk out of camp. And I ain't never wantin' to see your face again. Ya understand?

"I tried to help ya out, bein' that you were a boy, like my own. Then I tried to help ya 'cause Tommy took a liken' to ya. But this, there is no excuse for this prank. I want ya out, tonight!"

Alex stood with his arms folded across his chest and grinned at Gus. After the Push left, Alex walked over to Gus and said, "This ain't finished yet, Mr. Readin' Man."

Alex went into the kitchen and left Gus standing alone. What am I going to do? wondered Gus. Where am I going to go?

Gus was glad to have some time to himself when he went to the barn to milk Maw. He needed to think things through. When he returned to the cookshack he spent the rest of the morning avoiding Alex as much as he could. And Alex was always hanging around Addie so Gus couldn't talk to her about what had happened.

As dinnertime approached, Gus thought he would be able to talk with Tommy while they loaded the wagon. Maybe he could help him some way.

When the clanking of the wagon came from the barn, Gus started carrying baskets out the back door to wait for Tommy. Tommy pulled Dick and Jim around and jumped down from the wagon seat.

"There ya are, boy. I wanted to tell ya that the men are right fond of you this mornin' for the story ya read to 'em last night. If I have heard it once, I've heard it a dozen times that you have a talent for books." Tommy smiled so big his mustache rolled flat to his nose.

Gus silently put the baskets in the back of the wagon and walked over to Tommy.

"What's botherin' ya, boy? Ya look like ya lost your last friend."

Tommy was surprised when Gus told him what had happened. "Ya know, boy, since it has started to snow, I can tell the boss I'm gonna take the rig out ta-night to get the boys use to the white stuff. I can get ya into the settlement. If I drive all night, I can be back around sunup."

Gus's eyes filled with tears and his head dropped low. Just then Alex came out of the cookshack with his arms full of baskets.

"Hey, boy, you still have the day to work to pay for my boots. Get a move on or I'll tell my pa."

"Ya button your lip, ya troublemaker," responded Tommy. "If it weren't for you . . . ."

"Tommy!" snapped Addie who stood in the doorway. "The food's gettin' cold. Lend me a hand."

Gus knew Tommy shouldn't be talking that way to Alex who might encourage his father to fire the barn boss too.

Tommy patted Gus on the back, "Ya don't worry, I'll get ya set up in a boardin' house at the settlement. Maybe ya can find a job there. A boy who can read and who's got learnin' has a future."

Tommy helped Addie with the soup and coffeepots, and they spoke quietly between themselves.

"Gus," called Tommy. "I want ya to get in the wagon. You'll be back in about two and a half hours. Addie and I talked it over. You're going into the woods with me ta-day to deliver dinners."

"He can't go," demanded Alex. "That's my job. It's not fair. He can't go!"

"Look, ya mean-faced, spiteful little child, this here rig belongs to me personally—not to the camp and not to your father. I have a job to do, and I want the help of Gus here. Not you! Do ya understand me? Did ya hear me?"

Alex stood for a minute staring at Tommy giving him a dirty, mean look. "Yeah, I understand you, you son-of-an-Irishman," he yelled. "I understand you're gonna be takin' the long walk out of camp along with this dummy!"

Alex stormed off in the direction of the camp office.

"Tommy," said Addie, "Ya shouldn't have talked that way to the boy. Ya know his father will have your job."

"Addie, there comes a time when a person has to stand up for what he believes is right in this world. And Addie, my girl, I thought it was my time to stand up."

Addie smiled proudly at Tommy for what he had done.

Just then, Alex came stomping across the yard with his father following. "Tommy," bellowed the Push. "I hear we have another problem concerning the boy."

"No problem, sir," said Tommy, "I just felt I had to say my mind. And I want the boy to see the cuttin' ground since he has to be leavin' the camp. Leavin', I might add, because of a prank that was no fault of his."

"Now why in God's green earth would you want this boy to see the cuttin' ground? There will be no chance this boy will ever work in a lumber camp again. Word travels fast about troublemakers, and nobody wants one around."

'That's for sure," said Addie as she stood in the kitchen door listening.

"You be mindin' your mouth, woman, and get back to work!" shouted the Push.

"But sir, the boy...," said Tommy.

"There's no buts about this, Tommy. And furthermore, I think these two young 'uns still have somethin' to settle between them. Tommy, I want Alex to take your rig to deliver the dinners, and I want Gus to go along with him—alone.

"What has to be settled between these two should best be settled outside of camp. Maybe then, all this trouble will be over once and for all."

Addie slammed the backdoor of the kitchen as she left in disgust.

Gus swallowed hard. Here we go again, he thought.

"Ya-hooo," yelled Alex. "Let me at 'im."

"But sir, the roads are all rutted because of the frost and snow. The horses, they are spooky right now 'cause of that cougar that's been hangin' around. Sir, I don't think that the . . . ."

"That's right, Tommy, but it's not your job to think. It's only your job to take orders. Now if ya can't do what you've been told, then maybe you and your team better leave camp with the boy ta-night. Besides, you're always braggin' about how smart those horses of yours are. You say they know the tote road front and back, and they're more surefooted than my oxen. Here's your chance to prove it."

Tommy stood silent and moved away from the rig, handing the reins to Alex.

"Alex," said the Push, "I don't want you back in this camp 'til this trouble is settled. Ya understand?"

"Yes sir, Pa, I understand," said Alex with a rat grin on his face.

"Ya drive me rig with respect, ya hear me, Alex?" said Tommy. Alex ignored Tommy and jumped up onto the bench seat, whipping the horses' reins in the air with excitement.

"Another thin', Tommy," said the Push. "About that there cougar spookin' the horses. I've been thinkin' about that cat. Ya know, it's came to my attention that ya been feedin' that stinkin' bear lots of leftovers. Food the men could eat.

"I believe that there cougar can smell the food around the bear, or he wouldn't be sniffin' around. That's why I want ya ta get rid of that bear. Then maybe your horses wouldn't be so skitterish." The Push grinned at Tommy.

"Well, sir, ya know it's 'bout time to turn Napoleon loose to find a den for winter . . . ."

"Turn him loose? Man, don't you see what I'm gettin' at here? That bear can't be turned loose, Irish. Why, he'd be raidin' the camp for food. He's more man than bear now, 'cause of all the coddling. I want him shot!"

"NO!" yelled Gus, who had tried to stay out of the way until then. "Ya can't shoot Napoleon. I won't let you shoot him!"

"Ya won't let me shoot him, boy?" questioned the Push. "I don't rightly think ya got a say in the matter, you miserable little troublemaker. Now get yourself on the wagon and get out of here."

"Tommy, ya can't shoot him. He's my friend," pleaded Gus.

"Tommy, go get your gun and get the job done, now!" demanded the Push.

Gritting his teeth, Tommy stared hard at his boss, then walked off in the direction of the barn.

"Alex, get goin' and don't come back 'til things are settled. Ya hear?"

Tommy came back from the barn with his gun in his hand and went to where Napoleon stood chained to the tree.

Gus watched as the bear hopped up on his back legs and called to his friend, thinking he had brought him food.

Tommy unchained the bear and pulled him toward the woods on the chain.

"Tommy, don't do it," called Gus from the wagon.

"He'll do it all right, or he's fired," said Alex who was pulling on the reins, trying to control Dick and Jim.

"Come on, we got ourselves a job that needs lookin' after," insisted Alex.

"Alex, you be careful with that rig. I want those horses back in one piece and you, too," said the Push. "And Alex, do the job right!"

"Ya can count on me, Pa. Come on, dummy, let's go!"

Just as the wagon started to pull out, two shots rang out from the woods. "I guess the job is done now, wouldn't you say?" said Alex, laughing and directing his question to Gus.

Gus, who was ready to cry, stared out into the woods so that Alex wouldn't see how upset he was.

Alex slapped the back of the horses with the reins, and the horses bolted forward down the tote road toward the woods.

On their way out of camp, they passed Tommy, carrying Napoleon's chain in one hand and his gun in the other.

"You be careful with me rig, boy. The roads are hard and rutted. If ya aren't," he snarled, "I'll tan your hide."

Gus avoided looking at Tommy as they drove by. How could he shoot Napoleon just like that? he wondered.

Alex slapped the backs of the horses again and they started pulling faster. "**Haw**! Haw! Come on, Jim. Come on, Dick. **Gee**!"

The horses' ears lay flat at hearing the new voice at the reins and great puffs of steaming air blew from their flaring nostrils.

The wagon creaked as it wobbled back and forth on the rough road. No sooner had they rounded the curve out of camp when Alex slapped the reins again. The horses started to pick up speed.

Gus, bumping around on the wagon seat, leaned from one side to the other. Trying not to show fear, he held tightly to the side of the seat.

"Gee! Haw! Haw!" called Alex, slapping the horses again. This time, the horses, not used to the harsh treatment, reared up in their harnesses, throwing the wagon back. Then they took off running down the rutted road.

Gus held on tight and ducked back against the seat while Alex held tight to the reins. The food baskets and pots of coffee in the wagon slammed against each other. Soup sloshed out, and Gus, holding tight with one hand, reached back to keep a coffee pot from spilling.

Just then, from out of the woods, something dashed in front of the wagon.

The horses, swerved and then reared up in their harness, pawing at the sky and screeching in fright. The wagon was wrenched and thrown over on its side.

Gus went flying from the wagon, slamming hard against a tree and landing in a pile of dinner baskets and hot pots. The coffee he had tried to hold in the wagon scalded him as it spilled on his hands.

Gus was hurt and shaken. His hands were red and burned from the hot coffee. Lying on the ground for a minute, he tried to collect his thoughts. He could feel a goose egg forming on the back of his head where he had hit the tree.

Feeling a little dizzy, Gus struggled to get to his feet. When he finally caught his balance, he looked around. What a mess!

The wagon was on its side with the wheels still spinning. There were boxes and baskets and pots of food everywhere. But Alex was nowhere to be seen.

The horses, Dick and Jim, lay on their sides, still chained to the wagon. Kicking and whinnying, they struggled to get to their feet. Gus watched them, wondering if they were injured.

"Gus, Gus, help me! I can't move," cried a voice. It was Alex.

Looking around the wreckage, Gus found Alex with his foot pinned under the wagon near the seat.

"The horses. . .stop the horses from moving," cried Alex. "They keep moving the wagon on my foot."

Gus limped to the front of the wagon to see what he could do. The horses were wildly trying to pull free, but they seemed to be OK.

I've got to help them, thought Gus. He could see the harness chain still attached to a large bolt on the wagon tongue. Crawling into the wreckage behind the kicking horses, Gus unclipped the horses' chains with his scalded hands, allowing them to free themselves.

Struggling to get to their feet, the two horses, still in harness, righted themselves and turned, snorting and running together in the direction of the camp. The chains, dragging behind them made a terrible noise along the rutted, snowy ground.

Gus crawled over the tongue of the wagon to where Alex lay. His foot was caught fast beneath the wagon. Gus, gathering all his strength, tried to lift the wagon.

"I can't do it, Alex," cried Gus. Looking down at his hands he could see tiny blisters starting to form from his burns. "I've got to go get help. I've got to get back to camp."

Alex began crying loudly. "My foot, my foot, I can't feel my foot!" he sobbed. "Please help me! I'm gonna die! Help me!"

Just then, from out of the corner of his eye, Gus saw something moving cautiously through the woods. Turning slowly in the direction of the movement, he could see. It was the cougar¹

That's what scared the horses, thought Gus.

The cat now called out in a ferocious snarl, hissing at Gus when he looked in its direction.

Standing very still Gus watched the cat. Alex began moaning loudly. "Gus, Gus ya got to help me! I can't feel my foot! Gus, if ya help me, I'll tell everyone it was my fault about the fight. And I put the syrup on my boots so that stupid bear would eat them and you'd get kicked out of camp. I'll tell them everything!"

The cougar, crouching in the woods, stared at Gus but kept its distance. Then it began to pace and move closer, slinking from behind one tree to the next.

"Gus! Gus! Did ya hear me! I'll tell them everything! Go get help!" hollered Alex.

The cat, in a low, deep pitch, began to growl as Alex yelled louder and louder.

"Alex, shut up! The cougar's out there!" said Gus. Gus picked up a rock with his blistered hands and threw it as well as he could into the woods toward the cat.

"Gus? Gus? Where is it?" urged Alex.

"Alex, you better be quiet before that cat comes over here and eats you."

Gus searched the woods, looking for the cougar. It had disappeared. He listened for the cat's growl. There was nothing but silence.

Then from behind a tree, Gus could see the cat's long tail whipping back and forth, just like Betty's tail swished before she nailed him in the bunkhouse. The cougar poked its head out from behind the tree, its ears lying flat to its head and its yellow eyes staring wide and round at Gus. Slowly, it began to circle the wagon, slinking and swishing its tail.

Alex tried to lift himself up to look for the cat. Unable to, he dropped back. "Gus," he begged, "Gus, get me out of here!"

"Shh . . .," whispered Gus as he watched the cat. "Lie still."

For the moment Gus had forgotten about his blistered hands and about his head that pounded from the goose-egg bump. He tried to distract the cat by throwing another rock.

Taking aim, he threw the rock which slammed up against a tree. The thud echoed in the woods. The cougar moved from its position by the tree and circled closer to the boys, roaring out a great call that sent chills down Gus's spine.

"It's gonna eat us," yelled Alex. "It's gonna catch us and eat us."

Gus, who was not sure what to do, stood frozen, afraid even to breathe in case the cat decided to lunge.

Please, please, someone help, thought Gus. Please!

Just then, Gus thought he heard something in the woods. The sound seemed to be coming from behind the cougar. Maybe the men from the cuttin' grounds had heard them, Gus hoped.

The noise came closer and closer, as if someone was crashing slowly through the woods. The big cat turned and hissed, but Gus still couldn't see who it was.

Then, trampling out of the brush, came Napoleon. "It's Napoleon! It's Napoleon!" yelled Gus. "Tommy didn't shoot him! He didn't shoot Napoleon!" shouted Gus.

Napoleon, standing in the woods, rose up on his back feet, threw his head in the air, and made a dreadful howl.

The cougar turned to face its enemy. It jumped back, swatting its dangerous paw in the direction of the bear. Hissing, the cat crouched. The hair on the back of its neck stood tall. With its back arched it walked sideways, around the bear, not taking its eyes from Napoleon for one second.

Napoleon came down on all fours and faced the cat. Opening his mouth wide he swung his head from side to side, showing his long, sharp teeth. Napleon growled in a tone Gus had never heard before. It was deep and threatening.

The cougar, with his ears flat, recoiled and turned, running off into the woods as fast as it could.

"All right, Napoleon!" cheered Gus. "Napoleon scared the cougar away," Gus yelled to Alex.

Alex, who was terrified, lay on the ground with a dazed look in his eyes.

Just then, a shot rang through the woods. Gus could see men running down the tote road from the camp.

"Look it's Tommy and the men," shouted Gus, swinging his blistered hands into the air.

Tommy was the first one to reach the boys. He grabbed Gus and gave him a hug. "Ya all right, boy? Ya had me scared half to death when the horses came back to the barn without ya. It was a smart thing to do, turnin' those horses loose. They came right to me. I knew there was trouble. Are ya all right, boy?"

"I'm all right, but Alex is caught under the wagon. And the cougar, it came out of the woods and Napoleon . . . . Tommy, you didn't shoot Napoleon. He came out of the woods and went after the cat. He saved us, Tommy. Napoleon saved us."

The men, looking toward the woods, could see Napoleon who stood on his back legs and sniffed the air as he watched them. Then as if he understood that everything was fine, he turned and, on all fours, loped back into the woods.

The Push who joined the men, helped to lift the wagon off Alex's foot.

"Pa, that bear, Napoleon, he saved us! And Gus . . . Gus, he kept throwing rocks at that big cat trying to scare it away! That cat could see me, Pa. He was coming after me. And Napoleon and Gus, they both scared that cat away."

"Well, Irish," said the Push, "Ya just didn't have the guts, did ya?"

"Sir?"

"Ya didn't have the guts to follow orders and kill that bear like I told ya to, did ya?"

"No sir, " responded Tommy.

"And I'm glad ya didn't! You're a good man Tommy, me boy. You're a good man." The Push reached out and slapped Tommy across the back.

"Boy," said the boss turning to Gus. "That there bear friend of yours will always be welcome at camp for a handout. Won't he, Alex?"

Alex, who was now free from the wagon lay on the ground and rubbed his swollen foot.

"Pa . . . Pa . . . there's something I got to tell ya. Pa, you know when the men got into that fight . . ."

"Not now, boy," said the Push as he bent down and picked his son up in his arms. "We got to get this foot tended to, then we can talk.

"Boy, for helping my son here, I guess all is forgiven . . . . It might be best though, that you go help Tommy in the barn from now on. You and Alex just don't seem to get along.

"Ain't that right, son? said the Push directing his question to Alex.

Alex didn't say anything more as his father carried him back to camp.

"Ya know," said Tommy turning to Gus, "if ya hadn't turned those horses loose, there's no tellin' what might have happened to ya, boy. Ya done good ta-day, ya done real good."

"It was Napoleon, Tommy, he saved us," said Gus weakly. Gus was starting to feel dizzy, and he needed to sit down.

Tommy could see how badly Gus's hands were blistered and knew he was in no condition to walk back to camp. Scooping him up over his shoulder, Tommy carried his young friend back to camp.

Chapter 13
The Hero

Gus couldn't remember what happened to him after that. All he knew was that when he woke up, he could hear Addie gently talking to him. He had a cool cloth lying across his forehead and his hands were lightly covered with bandages.

"Gus . . . Gus . . . open your eyes, son. Open your eyes. Everything is all right now."

Gus opened his eyes and there, standing before him was, not Addie, but his mother.

Trying to sit up, Gus felt dizzy and eased himself back onto the bed. He blinked, the lights seemed so bright. "Where am I?" he asked weakly.

Opening his eyes again, he could see he was in the hospital. There, standing beside his mother was Tommy.

"Tommy, how did I get back?" questioned Gus.

"Hey, kiddo, how ya feeling? I don't suppose you know this, but you are a real hero at the White Pine School," said Mr. Kristie who was dressed in a plaid shirt. The curl was out of his bushy mustache.

"You know, Gus, if you hadn't gotten out of that bathroom and pulled the fire alarm when you did, I hate to think what would have happened. As it was, it was a real mess."

"Tommy, how did I get back?" asked Gus.

"Oh, Gus. You must have breathed in too much smoke from that awful fire," said his mother. "You poor thing. Are you all right?"

Gus began to remember. He remembered Alex or Al in the bathroom and the lighter and the paper towels.

The lumberjack camp must have all been a dream. A crazy dream! Gus looked down at his bandaged hands. This couldn't have happened with the black lead, could it? he wondered.

"The wastebasket, Gus, don't you remember? It was red hot from the fire. You burned your hands on the wastebasket trying to move it away from the paper towel holder," said his mother.

"What about Alex? What happened to Alex?" questioned Gus.

"You mean Al?" asked Mr. Kristie. "You don't need to worry about Al any more. After he started the fire he ran down the hall toward the front entrance of the school. He tripped on the steps going out and sprained his ankle pretty badly. He was so scared he admitted he had a lighter and started the fire."

"Gus, Al even told Mr. Kristie why you and he are always fighting. I understand now why you didn't want to tell me. You didn't want to hurt my feelings," said his mother.

Gus felt good to hear his mother say she understood.

"Al is down in the emergency room, getting his ankle bandaged, Gus," said Mr. Kristie. "I don't think he's going to be bothering you anymore."

Just then, there was a tap at the door. It was Mr. Knowles, the Big Push. And he was pushing Al in a wheelchair; his ankle was all bandaged and sticking out in front of him. In his lap was a large paper sack. Mr. Knowles shoved the door open and wheeled Al in, but before he could get all the way through the door, it swung back and bumped Al's bandaged foot.

"Ouch!" he yelled in pain.

"Gus," said Knowles, ignoring Al. "This young man has something to say to you. Don't you, Al?"

The door opened again and there stood Al's parents. "Allen, don't you have something to say to Gus?" they urged.

Al hung his head. When he looked up, Gus could see Al had been crying. "I'm sorry Gus," Al said without really looking at him. "I'm sorry for everything."

Al's parents, standing at the back of the room, spoke up. "Mrs. McCarty, we are sorry for what has happened to your son because of Allen.

"We want you to know, Gus will never be bothered by Allen again. Isn't that right, Allen?

"And as far as the hospital bills go, we insist on paying them."

Annie McCarty nodded her head, "Thank you, I appreciate that."

"Allen," said Mr. Knowles, "don't you have something to give to Gus?"

"Yes sir," and Al handed Gus the paper bag that sat in his lap.

"This gift is from Allen and myself," said Mr. Knowles, "for pulling the fire alarm and saving the school.

"I hope you like this, Gus. There wasn't much of a selection down at the gift shop. Allen, somehow, thought you would like this."

Gus's mother helped Gus remove the gift from the bag. It was the most perfect gift Gus could have ever wanted.

"Napoleon!" cried Gus. "It's Napoleon. Al, how did you know?"

Gus took a hand-carved bear out of the bag and patted its head with his bandaged hands.

Pleased by his reaction, Mr. Knowles smiled. "Well, I suppose we should be going and let Gus get his rest so he can get back to school."

Al's parents agreed as they pushed his wheelchair from the room with Mr. Knowles following.

Gus examined the wooden bear. It was like seeing his old friend Napoleon again. Dreams are really weird, thought Gus.

"You know, Annie . . . Mrs. McCarty," said Mr. Kristie. "I don't want you to worry about Gus getting behind in school. I'll stop by with his work so he can keep up with his class-mates."

"But Mr. Kristie, I couldn't ask you to do that. You're a busy man," said Annie McCarty.

"There's no one waiting for me at home. It would be my pleasure to help Gus," said Mr. Kristie with a twinkle in his eye.

"'Oh by the way, Gus, Al is also suspended from school for a week. And it looks like he will have to go to summer school because he's skipped so many classes. I thought you would like to know.

"Maybe when you start feeling better, you and your mom would like to go on a picnic behind my farm. We can make it kind of educational," said Tom Kristie as he smiled at Annie.

"You see, behind my farm there used to be an old lumberjack camp. I like to go out there on the weekends and look for all sorts of interesting things. Why, I've found old buckles from horse harnessses and a great looking metal chain, hooked to a tree. Once I even found the parts to what looked like an old cookstove."

Gus smiled up at his mother, "It sounds great. Mom, can we go?"

Annie smiled at her son, "Well, sure, but you will have to get better first, OK?"

"Annie, why don't we let the boy get some rest so he can go home in the morning? Would you like to go have a cup of coffee with me in the dining hall?" asked Mr. Kristie."We can talk about Gus's schoolwork."

Annie McCarty smiled at Mr. Kristie with a twinkle in her eyes, and Mr. Kristie smiled back with a grin so big, his bushy mustache lay flat against his nose.

amen corner. A corner of the bunkhouse where the old-timers sat or entertainers told their stories.

as easy as falling off a log. A term that came from lumbermen, or river drivers, standing and walking on logs as they floated them down rivers during the log drives.

axe man. A lumberjack whose main job was notching trees using an axe.

backfire. A fire set in front of a large forest fire to create a barren place that would stop or slow down the main fire.

baker. A large stove that had an oven.

balloon. A bedroll.

barkeater. A lumberjack or worker at a sawmill.

barn boss. Person whose duty it was to care for the horses and stables.

barn boy. A barn boss's helper.

bed down. To move into a logging camp.

belly burglar. A bad cook.

big as a bear and lazy as two. A lazy lumberjack.

Big Push. Boss.

black lead. Coffee.

blue jacket. Body lice.

blue jay. Someone who works on the tote road.

board foot. A measurement for logs and lumber. It is a board one inch thick, twelve inches wide, and twelve inches long.

body lice. Small, wingless bugs that bite. They were common in lumber camps.

boot grease. A mixture of animal fat, beeswax, and a little lamp black (soot from oil lamps) used to waterproof boots.

box up the dough. To knead bread.

break a ham string. To work with speed, or to do one's best.

breech loader. Bunks built along the walls so that lumberjacks had to crawl in from the side.

brolo. A large stick or club for pounding horses to make them pull harder or to obey orders.

bull pen. Another name for bunkhouse.

buckwheater. New man in the camp.

cackleberries. Eggs. Also called hen fruit.

Canadian grays. Warm woolen socks.

chew. Chewing tobacco.

cookee. Any kind of cook's helper.

cookhouse. The kitchen and dining room in a logging camp.

cooking stove. A large cast iron, wood-burning stove with six or more pot openings.

cookshack. A cabin where cooking was done.

cootie cage. A bunk or bed in lumber camp.

corks. Spikes.

corker. Someone or something astonishing or excellent.

corking. Driving spikes into a horse's shoe to prevent slipping on the ice.

clod-hoppers. Heavy or clumsy shoes or boots.

crawler. A louse.

critter. An animal of some type.

crumb chaser. A cook's helper.

crummy. Covered with lice.

cut plug chewing tobacco. A solid piece of chewing tobacco.

daylight in the swamp. A wake-up call for lumberjacks.

deacon bench. Seat or bench near the bunks.

dinnering out. Having a meal in the woods. Dinner was the name for the noon meal at that time in history.

doorknobs. Biscuits.

douse the glim. Lights out!

dresses. Horse harnesses.

fell. To cut down trees.

feed bag. A nose bag for a horse.

flappers. Pancakes.

gee and haw. Commands used by oxen and horse drivers to indicate to the animal which way to turn. Gee means to turn to the right; haw means to turn to the left.

greenhorn. A newcomer, or someone without experience.

greybacks. Lice.

grub. Food.

hair pounder. A horse teamster.

hay-burner. Horse.

hay feathers. A mattress or pillow made of hay instead of feathers.

jerk the hash. Serve the food.

muzzle loader. A bed that has to be entered by crawling in the end.

logging horses. Heavy horses used in logging. Many weighed one ton. They were generally purchased from Iowa, Illinois or Pennsylvania farms. Also called old plugs, karrons, rocking horses. The average life of horses used for logging was three to five years.

log road. A sled or tote road.

long johns. Heavy wool underwear with long sleeves and legs, often red in color.

long sweetening. Sugar.

long walk. Get fired.

louse cage. A hat.

lousy camp. A logging camp infested with body and head lice.

off his feed. Sick

outhouse. A shack containing a pit toilet.

pants rabbits. Body lice.

pratties. Potatoes.

road monkey. A man who kept the tote road in good shape.

roll in. Go to bed.

scratch-my-back. Saw fiddle.

sinkers. Donuts.

slashings. Brush left from lumbering.

snoose. A slang word made up from the Danish word for snuff or tobacco.

squeeze box. Small accordion.

stack. A pile of flappers, or pancakes.

store bought. Fancy clothes.

swamp grass. Coarse hay cut from a marsh or swamp.

Swedish brain powder. The ashes left in a pipe after smoking.

Scandanavian dynamite. A tar ball left in a pipe.

teamster. Man who drove a team in a logging operation.

toque. A knit cap worn by some jacks.

tote road. A main road in and out of a camp.

vagabond. Bum.